THE DEADLANDS
SUMMER 2024

THE DEADLANDS

ISSUE 35, SUMMER 2024

ISBN-13: 979-8-89116-007-1

psychopomp.com

For more information, contact Psychopomp: ask@psychopomp.com

This publication is a work of fiction. Names, characters, places, and incidents either are products of the authors imaginations or are used fictitiously. Any resemblance to actual persons, living or dead, events, or locales is entirely coincidental.

Publisher: Sean Markey
Editor in Chief: E. Catherine Tobler
Poetry Editor: Nicasio Andres Reed
Social Media: Felicia Martínez
Art Director: inkshark
Nonfiction Editor: David Gilmore
Necromancer at Large: Amanda Downum
Copy Editor: Laura Blackwell
Designer: Christine M. Scott
Cover: "At the All Of This Book," by Inkshark

The Deadlands is distributed quarterly by:
Psychopomp
PO Box 36
Woodbury, VT 05681

Subscriptions can be purchased at weightlessbooks.com. Individual issues can be obtained by joining our Patreon (with many deadly perks).
Join here: thedeadlands.com/patreon

SUMMER 2024

fiction

...CAL IMPACTS OF
...N: A FIELD STUDY

Corey Farrenkopf

EDITOR'S NOTE

MAY YOU LIVE IN INTERESTING TIMES, THEY SAID.

May you publish interesting things, they did not say—but it's what we do, what *The Deadlands* has done from our first issue, and here we are with Issue #35.

This issue feels unlike others before it, and so this little note: You might want to hydrate before you jump in. Have a snack. Stretch those limbs. Check your heart—is it there, is it ready? Make sure your chair is attached to the floor. Turn the phone off. Grab the tissues. Tie your shoelaces or hitch up your socks.

This is a heavy issue, dealing with our extremely modern world. It covers topics such as meat processing, the "N-word," and the decades-long genocide in Gaza. The terrain will be difficult, but it will be worthwhile. Let us go into this together and come out on the other side better than when we went in.

E. Catherine Tobler
July 2024

TABLE OF CONTENTS

TABLE OF CONTENTS

SPAWN RED MEAT ARACHNID

Chris Panatier

He occupies the office above the bleeding floor,
Pacing, a shadow. Pulled blinds, obscure.
Below, his opus: his system, perfected.
Efficient. Patented. Robotic. Protected.

A column of machines do the slaughter-line dance,
His monument to rendering lucre from flesh.
Bolt guns to bleeding. Flay, evisceration,
Split guts, cling wrap. Monetization.

The man blows on coffee, licks his dried lips,
Meeting all the metrics of beef cows per shift.
Twenty-four thousand two hundred and six,
Dividend payment, *steak*-holder fix.

Demand is increasing, and he's the supply,
Just a minute 'tween death and prepackaged-to-buy.
They moo, they squeal, they huff, stomp a hoof,
Cacophonous to silent. Suspended on hooks.

Fevered snouts cast 'round. Panic in the line,
Swollen viscera, infection. Forklift tine.
If they walk, you can slaughter, say the regulations.
Reach down, pump lever. IV medications.

End of the trail, shorn skin in a stack,
Runnel of blood, electrical crack.
The pile—it shakes, vibrates, and moves,
Congeals, limbs form. Life. Looms.

Six legs, then eight, crooked horns unwind,
Crawling starfish of meat. A new raging mind.
Carcass tartar. Eyes form a crown,
Scan for the man who put them all down.

Ribs jut like claws from marbled toe,
Hanging from rafters, spy silhouette, *go*.
Lurching hulk, methane rasp,
Bursting wall. Broken glass.

The beef finds its mark and away he is carried,
Within bosom of meat, he's embraced and he's buried.
Eyes swivel 'round, see the warehouse in back,
Find man's old equipment, all dusty and black.

No robots, no machines, no murderous code,
Just steel rods and chains, and shackles. Cold.
A calf, he is laid to the skinning cradle,
Mewling ruminant. Supper table.

Transection. Open. Hide pulled away,
Fever dreams come. Clasp hands: *Pray.*
Beef stands over. Man whinnies shame.
Sinews ascend, bone breathes vein.

Meal now dressed, cow spider gives birth,
Eyes draw wide to edge of girth.
Strip-steak womb. The mound opens up,
Caldera of flesh. A tear. Erupt.

They pour to the floor. Meatballs with teeth
Swarm up his limbs on eyelash feet.
Easy bits first: cheeks, then lips,
Armpits, earlobes. Fingertips.

He bleeds, but he lives for one more breath,
Then the beef mouth smiles, declares: *Death.*
Sated and strong, her children congeal,
Spawn red meat arachnid down slaughter-line trail.

Leap to machines, tear wire from root,
Robots topple. Crashing. Mute.
Rush the corral. Broken pipe,
Animals flee to waxing night.

Engulfed in flame, slaughterhouse fire,
For the man and his system: funeral pyre.
Beef mother counts heads. Brain makes a list,
All twenty-four thousand two hundred and six.

THE ECOLOGICAL IMPACTS OF RESURRECTION: A FIELD STUDY

Corey Farrenkopf

FEW species other than humans bury their dead. A number of mammals undertake death rituals or practice forms of post-mortem grieving, but few will place a body in the ground with intent. Elephants stand watch over their deceased for days. Chimpanzees have been known to carry their infant dead for months after they pass. Even dolphins and giraffes practice varied forms of mourning, but most don't inter the bodies. Which was why the otters in the forested backwoods of Hubbardston, Massachusetts, were so important to my father's studies.

Sitting in a hunter's blind with their dad by the side of a marshy river for twelve-hour days was not how most girls wanted to spend the summer before freshman year of college, but there I was, swatting blackflies off my bare arms.

The scent of damp rot wafted off the river as our polyethylene tenting shivered with the breeze. We had nestled the collapsible structure into a copse of birches three days before. The shade was not enough to fight the August heat. Sweat clung to the backs of my knees and beneath my bra. Dad sat beside me, squinting through a pair of binoculars, jotting messy notes into his journal as I drew cartoon variations of the otters attending a Victorian tea party.

My father was a professor of Ethology at the University of Massachusetts Amherst, focusing on the study of death rituals and burial behavior in mammals and their intersections with human traditions. He said he was going to write his next paper on the otters, maybe even his next book.

Judging by the nearly incomprehensible notes and the large collection of question marks, it looked like he would struggle to fill the pages.

Nothing had happened since we arrived. Just a few families of cute brown river otters swimming into view, then out of view, occasionally playing in the mud on the river bank, which was adorable, occasionally eating a small fish or frog, which was less so.

At no point did they break out the shovels and start unearthing a crypt, much to my father's dismay.

Two weeks before, Aunt Claire left a voicemail on our home answering machine.

...two little otter paws sticking out of the ground just like my neighbor said, praying to the sky. The rest of the body was buried, otter prints all around. They must be burying their dead. I told Bill to keep quiet until you could come take a look. I know how competitive your research is. Sorry I haven't been in touch lately. It's just hard, you know?

I did know. Mom had been dead for thirteen years. I could barely remember her face or the sound of her voice. Dad always tried to remind me about her. The blonde hair I didn't inherit. The floral mist that seemed to follow her around. Her dark humor and artistic tendencies that allegedly mirrored my own.

I often asked myself if that's why my father's career shifted, every choice in his life tracing back to her death.

Before the accident he studied the foraging behaviors of wild pigs, teasing out connections to the truffle trade in Italy. But now the only buried things he obsessed over were bodies and their implications. *If animals care for the dead, it could mean they also believe in the hereafter... An animal kingdom variation of heaven? Who knows what they might actually know...* I'd sat in on his lectures, listening to rambles on potential elephant gods and crow hell, as if it all held a clue to his own personal mystery, a hidden path back to Mom.

His desire was blatant in every word, even if his students couldn't hear it.

As each year passed, his hypothesis grew more extreme and improbable.

Just because other mammals actively dealt with death, it didn't mean they believed in God or ghosts or eternal salvation, but I never brought it up. Dad paid the bills with his macabre theories and professor evals.

Kids loved hearing about spooky dogs sleeping on the graves of their masters and how horses hold viewings for their dead.

He always got high ratings.

"Can we head back to Aunt Claire's?" I asked once the last of the otters disappeared into the current.

"Jeany, weren't you listening this morning?" he replied without dropping his binoculars.

"I thought so, why?"

"We're staying the night. If the otters aren't burying their dead during the daytime, maybe it has to do with the phases of the moon. I saw some roadkill on the way in. It's not like they have an excuse not to."

The marshy, chest-deep river was bisected at several points by a rural highway. Two lanes, no divider, forty-five-mile-an-hour speed limits. On the drive in, I'd seen a singular dead otter spread out on the beer can-littered shoulder. I'd read reports about their untimely deaths along the roadway, how they just weren't quick enough to avoid squealing tires. I scanned every accident report for the area and was honestly surprised we didn't see more woodland casualties, raccoons and foxes and deer. It was a high fatality three-point-five miles for any animal. The surrounding forest of moss-draped trees pressed up to the asphalt in some places, visibility low.

This was all information I gathered for my father's potential book.

He needed all the filler he could get to meet the appropriate page requirement.

We'd dig wherever we could.

"But I didn't bring a sleeping bag," I said, stowing my drawings beneath my beach chair.

"You have to make sacrifices for science," he replied with a smile.

Dad still believed I wanted to follow in his footsteps and become an ethologist. Yes, I was interested in science, in helping others understand the world around them, but I preferred hybridizing my interests. Medical illustration. Wildlife illustration. Botanical illustration. Almost anything blankety-blank-science-related-illustration would do.

"Yeah, yeah, yeah," I replied, pulling a pair of sunglasses from my backpack, shading my eyes. "If that's the case, then I'm taking a nap. Wake me up when they start the burial procession."

"They don't do that, Jeany. You know…"

But I'd already stopped listening. If I wanted to avoid a migraine, I needed to get a little sleep.

The chimpanzees always got me. The thought of carrying your dead child around for weeks on end sounded like a nightmare. Continuing to groom them, pretending to teach them behavioral skills to survive. Whenever Dad talked about the behavior during his lectures, I imagined him carrying Mom's body around, combing her hair, performing disquieting ventriloquism whenever we went out for dinner.

Even if Mom's body wasn't actually present at every meal, leaning against Dad's shoulder for stability, she was there in spirit, speaking through my father's lips whenever he stood at the front of the lecture hall, going on about dolphins guarding their dead to make sure they arrived at the great beyond undisturbed.

Every decision he'd made since the accident thirteen years ago was aimed at an unattainable outcome.

He was still guarding her body the only way he knew how.

"What the hell."

I startled awake, my father leaning forward in his chair, squinting into the dark.

"Dad, what…" I began before he shushed me, raising a silencing finger.

My eyes were still fuzzed with sleep, vision through the open tent slit blurred. Fog drifted off the water. The landscape was more fitting for a cheap vampire movie than an ecological study. I squinted, wiping at my eyes until things came into focus.

I wished they hadn't.

Standing in the river was something akin to a man, bare to the waist, a pair of tattered black pants covering his lower half. Thinning silver hair fell to his shoulders, water-slick as if he'd just swum up from the depths. The issue with classification lay in his skin, or rather on it. Visible stretches of his chest and arms were crosshatched with what looked like strips of moss and animal hide, tufts of rabbit fur sewn here, what appeared to be a swath of a coyote's pelt stitched there.

I searched frantically around the blind for a weapon of any sort, eyes roving for protection, trying to not let my plastic beach chair whine beneath me. There was the shovel we used to unearth the first otter grave, my slightly sharpened pencils, and the cooler holding the leftovers from lunch. Nothing to strike from a distance.

My father's hand fell to my knee, gripping, establishing stillness.

"He hasn't seen us," my father whispered, leaning as close as he could to the blind's opening without sticking his head through. "Watch."

My heart convulsed in my throat. Everything about the sewn man told me to run, fight or flight reduced to a single option, but I fought to hold my breath. Dad had weird ideas about the afterlife, but in most things besides my mother, he was pure logic. If he didn't want us to move, I had to trust him.

The sewn man stepped from the river and climbed the muddy embankment, dropping into a squat over a flat section of earth. I hadn't noticed before, but he had something cradled in his arms. A tuft of fur, the white gleam of bone. I originally thought the otter had been another pelt composing the man's skin, but when he stood the little creature up on its hind legs, there was no denying it wasn't part of him.

There was something clearly wrong with the otter. Its back leg dragged while it walked, head drooping as if its neck was broken. Ridges of stitching coursed over its fur, small knobs of bone peering through the handiwork.

"That thing has to be…" I began.

"Dead. I know," my father replied. "Don't ruin this. Get your sketchbook."

I fished the papers from beneath my seat and began to draft the scene, the injured otter hobbling forward before it began to dig, the sewn man lingering in the background. The undead creature made quick work of the trench, hollowing out a hole big enough for its body. Then it lowered itself down into the earth, pawing at dirt piles left around the tomb's edge. The otter managed to cover itself completely until only its paws remained above the soil, twin boney antennae pointed toward the heavens.

The sewn man knelt at the water's edge and made a number of odd motions with his hands before stepping back into the river.

"Soon. Soon," he said, before submerging fully, silver hair disappearing into the fog. Only the kick of his feet against the water marked his passage.

My father and I sat in silence, as if waiting for a camera crew to emerge from the opposite shore, some B-list actor calling through a megaphone, letting us know we'd been punked. But the stillness was total, all-consuming. Only the brush of the current against the shore stirred the reeds.

"So, is that going in the paper?" I asked once the moment stretched too long.

"That is going in the *book*," my father replied. "But I think it's also more than that. Let me see the drawing."

I handed it over.

"Maybe that will be the cover," he said, smiling.

When most animals are caught burying their dead, it's often a journalistic mistake, completely unrelated to an animal's belief in the afterlife. A number of years ago, a video went around the internet of a dog burying another dog. It was shared endlessly, people captioning the clip with big-hearted comments about how they must have been best friends, that the living must mourn the dead. Many read like bad plots to Hallmark movies, or a sad intro for a Pixar flick, but the truth was, dogs instinctively bury meat and bones.

The dog was most likely putting a meal aside, not honoring the dead, but that doesn't get many likes on social media.

People ignored the facts, blocking the few scientists who entered the fray trying to correct the script. Dad wrote an article on the phenomenon and the connection to his studies for *Nature,* but they never ran it. *Too esoteric,* they wrote back. *This won't pass peer review.*

When something didn't fit into a narrative, it got swallowed.

I didn't know what narrative the sewn man fit into, but I doubted anyone besides the *Weekly World News* was going to be interested.

Aunt Claire lived a few towns over in Fitchburg, in the same three-bedroom ranch she and my mother grew up in. She'd kept all the old photographs, smiling faces of my mother as a bespeckled blonde child, then a teenager with ill-advised bangs, peering out from behind faded glass. My father asked her to hang them in her guest room.

The bureau at the foot of the first twin mattress was a shrine to Mom, so many repeating faces staring out at you whenever you went to bed, all slowly aging toward the inevitable. I wanted to ask Aunt Claire if maybe she could tone it down, strip the memorial to its barest form, but somehow the shrine gave my father comfort, so I never voiced my complaint.

He stood before the array of photographs as I adjusted my sheets in the neighboring bed, pulling them up to my neck to ward off the chill from the A/C humming in the window.

"Dad, if you're going back tomorrow, which is a terrible idea, you really need your sleep," I whispered.

"You're not coming with me, Jeany? After a discovery like this?" His voice was distant as he ran a finger along the edge of the nearest photograph.

"You do you, but there's no way I'm going back out there."

"But this is the turning point in my career. Your mother would want you there with me."

"You can't put words in the mouths of the dead," I said, turning to face the wall, praying sleep would come quickly.

———

After a while, my father must have assumed I was out cold. He began to whisper to my mother's portraits.

We'll be like the crows, watching their dead. Just you wait…

He went on for what felt like forever, reciting pieces of old lectures, as if trying to reason through something, repeating statistics as if they were incantations. He spoke of plans I couldn't quite understand, logic not following from one word to the next. When I could no longer take his macabre monologue, I yawned, rolling over in my bed. The movement was enough to get him to stop talking, enough to bring back the quiet I so desperately needed.

My father muttered a quick *goodnight* before slipping into his bed.

I knew his words weren't meant for me, only the photographs lining the bureau. My mother's ghost was never far off.

———

"Do you remember that game you used to play with her?" my father asked, sitting inside the blind, the orange glow of sunset an hour past. The sky had settled into darkness. I told myself I wasn't going to come, that my father was on his own, but when eight o'clock rolled around and he hadn't replied to any of my texts, I took Aunt Claire's keys and drove through the neighboring towns to search for him.

I found my father in the same spot as yesterday, peering through binoculars into the dark, notebook closed as if he'd forgotten a pen.

"That doesn't really matter right now. We're leaving before that weirdo shows up," I said, standing just inside the blind's open entrance.

"Please, think back. This is important. You'll see. What game did you and your mother play?" my father asked again, lowering his binoculars, eyes refusing to meet my own. He looked beyond me, as if I weren't there.

"I don't know, like tag or something?"

"She used to call it 'Baby Possum.' You'd cling to her back as she jostled around the yard. It was your favorite."

I tried to remember the feeling of her body beneath mine, the way my fingers must have gripped her jacket as she half-heartedly attempted to shake me off, but nothing came. Our time together was a void, an unalterable emptiness. Nothing my father could say was going to bring her back for me.

"Honestly, I don't think I remember."

"Surprising. You asked her to play every day. I just keep thinking about what life would have been if she hadn't died. Opossums play dead, but it's never permanent."

"Is that going in your book too?"

"I'm not worried about the book anymore," my father replied as the sounds of feet sloshing through mud came from the riverbank.

The sewn man stepped from the water, the orange fur of a fox clutched to his chest, matted with blood, yards and yards of stitching coursing over its small body. Moonrise cast the river in a shifting skin of silver. Shadowed reflections of reeds and pale trees washed against the shore, the man a rotting silhouette of ink against the opaque backdrop. Like before, he knelt in the mud, helping the dead fox find its footing. Unlike the otter, the animal struggled to move, dragging itself more than walking.

"It's a short way, my friend. I'll be back soon," the man whispered to the fox, placing his hands underneath its shoulders, easing the weight off its paws. Something clicked as it moved, bone grinding against bone.

"Dad, we need to…" I began to say, before he pushed past me, out of the blind. I stumbled after him, straight into the birches, arms grasping a branch woven with brambles. Thorns cut into my flesh as I struggled to get untangled.

I swore, pulling myself free as my father snuck toward the sewn man's blind side, empty handed, as if he were going to try to catch him like Steve Irwin in one of the old episodes of *The Crocodile Hunter* we used to watch. He was almost to the sewn man when my father stepped on a rotting branch.

The sewn man looked up, turning as the fox continued to crawl along the shore, belly marking a snail trail in the mud. The sewn man tensed as if ready to lunge into the water, but he hesitated, eyes going wide, a closed-lip smile crossing his face. His gaze swiveled from my father to the blind, catching my eye in the copse of birch.

He had known we were there, had known we'd return.

My heart seized. A cold drip slipped down my spine.

My father circled, positioning himself between the man and the water, cutting off any escape route. He extended his arms, palms out, as if to show he meant no harm. Then he knelt, bowing in supplication.

The sewn man's lips parted, unveiling a number of mismatched teeth, molars and canines borrowed from other mouths. No words came out. Instead, he laughed, each huff like leaves rustling in the wind. He extended a patchwork hand, stroking my father's shoulder, almost lovingly.

I couldn't wait any longer.

I sprinted from where I stood in the trees, each heartbeat a heavy throb in my ear. My legs churned, the distance so much farther than it seemed. Time distorted, stretched to breaking. My father's words from the night before resurfaced: promises to my mother, promises of rebirth, of the next steps he needed to take.

I was beginning to realize what those next steps entailed.

As the revelation blossomed in my mind, my feet went out from under me, heels slipping through mud, the view of the river shifting to a view of the sky as I fell. Mud suctioned onto my back and legs, dampening my clothes, weaving into my hair. I'd almost made it. The fox was beside me, beginning to dig its own grave. The creature, unfazed by my sudden collapse, continued to excavate the earth with its broken forepaws, bones clicking together with each motion.

I fought to get up, but only made it to my knees. They were so close, but so far away, as if inhabiting a world removed from my own. The sewn man released my father's shoulder and walked to the river's edge, stepping in, beckoning him with an outstretched hand.

"Dad, don't. Mom's gone," I said, beginning to cry. "But I'm still here."

Without replying, he waded into the river.

"Dad…" I screamed, but he only shook his head, following the sewn man as he moved into the current, sinking up to his chest.

There was a moment when my father froze, looking at me over his shoulder. Both his head and the sewn man's head were just above the waterline, floating like twin buoys in the river. I was expecting a final goodbye, some well-wish or even an apology, but he said nothing, only turning back to the man leading him farther downstream. Then he began to paddle hard, legs kicking to keep up with his guide.

In the years since, I've seen my father swim away from me again and again, the memory stuck on a loop, choosing the possibility of his dead wife over the reality of his living daughter. I was frozen in that moment, clothes slick with muck and my own blood, the truth of what lay before me incomprehensible, dream logic refusing to align. I couldn't take my eyes off the river, off the dwindling dot that was the back of my father's head.

Then I heard the click of bone, the strain of broken paws tunneling beside me. I couldn't remember a single one of my father's lectures that contained a fox. Their burial practices were foreign to me, but so was everything else in that moment. I didn't know if it was shock, or detachment, but I dug my fingers into the cool mud, assisting the fox in unearthing its tomb as the moon climbed the sky, the river lapping at our backs, the kick of my father's feet fading into the night.

INVERSE REQUIEM

Abhinav

for Sakshi

YOUR face an oblong fact. Your hair a swirl of light in a jagged syntax. The curve of your laughter like a shot of caffeine in the mainline vein. This is how you look from the other side of my death—Your wrists torqued, shoulders hunched, your eyes a liquid curl of endless awe. You map the graveyard like a mouth does the memory of love; digressing along the diagonals— stumbling through the weeds to unfurl a nerve you didn't yet know existed. *What do they mean?* You asked me once, *The things you write— what are they a gesture of?* And I said I wanted to speak from outside of my death— clutch and claw at things beyond the clasp of language. And it isn't bad, to be honest; the ground eats all light and lets nothing through. Everyone is used to the quiet of it— lulled into sleep like a formless child. The mind outside the skull is just one— cold and liquid— membraned like a sheet of transparent glass. I get to walk in and out of your dreams and invent the past. There, the splash in the skyline from the day I met you, and the gust of breeze from the ocean in our backyard. The veins of the sidewalk spelling our names incorrectly. The sun slivered at the edges of the neem tree— the truncated symmetry of its scattered light and the unending crescendo of old-time Gods. The bravado and the fatigue of it all. Possibility piled up on possibility. The bright wild static of our childhood— the light spilling out of our hands like a litany of unsaid things. It's all here— everything we lost— like a river of unending quench. Memory has no margins here, the world winnows all at once and everything is water— nothing sinks. And yet I am always swimming towards you, gnawing against the current, nudging and nudging against the curve of things. Your voice an anchor at the wrong end of a very long tunnel and I twist and turn in my sleep, crush the maggots underneath— trying to find my way to the dream within the dream where we hold hands again.

RAISING AN ANCESTOR

Kay Mabasa

YOU'VE been angry for three full moons, but you don't know this, or rather you've forgotten this. There's a lot that you've forgotten. Such as who you are, or what it is that has befallen you. But this anger and state of forgottenness is all normal, it's expected.

You're in a vast darkness where the blackness of the ground mirrors the blackness of the air around you and the blackness of the sky that hangs above you. This I can safely say is what you do not know. Even if your memory were intact you would not know of this place, for it's foreign to you.

You walk in this darkness, or should I say you hover? Yes, you have feet, but they do not quite touch the ground, do they? And there have been times you've looked down at your feet and wondered at this, but not for too long, for your mind erases itself just as a thought occurs to you, and you forget what it was you were thinking of, or what it was that you were doing. And this is the true reason for your anger, that your mind doesn't work in the way that it should. But you don't know this, for you forget this very reason.

You forget that you forget.

Your memory is not as good as it used to be; in truth, your memory is dead. In fact, so many parts of you are dead. You don't know this, but you mourn for this memory of who and what you were.

It is cold in this black space, and your olive silk dress and gold sandals do nothing to aid this. There is something that you need that will help you keep warm, but you have not yet obtained it. So for now, you shiver as you hover through this night space and as you breathe out or open your mouth, clouds of mist come out.

There are others here with you. You're not alone. Their skin is ebon just like yours, and they have gray kinky curls like you, but theirs are set into various hairdos. They wear different clothes and shoes from you; some wear clothes with no shoes, while others wear no clothes or shoes. They are tall, short, lean, and some are plump, but one thing common about all of them is that they all smile at you. None of their faces are familiar; they're all strangers to you and yet they stare and smile at you. Some even wave, and others hug you.

When they talk to you, their words come out in a code that your mind fails to decipher. You try to talk to these strange faces, but what tumbles out are mumbles that even you do not understand, and you're not even sure what it was that you wanted to say to them.

You've forgotten how to speak.

Amused smiles appear on their faces when you try to talk. Their brown eyes watch you as if they were watching a child babbling. And when they see you get worked up, they rub your back in an attempt to soothe you. You feel like a child although you've forgotten what a child is, but that is how you feel: You're unable to crack the grownups' coded language.

Alone.

You feel alone in this vast night space that is filled with smiling strangers. Unable to speak to them or understand what it is they're saying, your questions of who you are, what it is that has happened to you, and where it is that you are, remain unanswered. And none can reassure you that soon your situation will change, for none can communicate this to you in a way that you would hear, understand, or remember.

Always, after they've rubbed your back, you leave them, and you're roiling in anger. You wander off into the night's emptiness until you forget what it was that had made you cross or drove you into the blackness. And so you wander back to the others, who aren't angry like you, but laugh in a drunken manner and embrace each other like old friends. And always, when you return, they stop for a moment and turn to you with their warm, welcoming smiles before they go back to their loud and strange conversations.

You change; like you had three full moons ago, but of course you've forgotten. You've forgotten the you of three full moons ago, the you that was in an incessant state of shock where everything around you had shocked you, where your forgetful mind shocked you when you tried to think of what it was you were thinking of or what it was that you were doing. And so now, no longer in shock and no longer angry, you're in a state of trying.

You're trying to fix things, trying to better yourself. It's not a conscious change; it's just your soul evolving, shaping itself to what it will eventually become.

So you try to decode the smiling strangers' speech, and there are times that you even laugh when they laugh. But it's a cold laugh; no joy lives in you, you're an empty husk. Each time you laugh with them, they stop laughing and turn to look at you with their warm smiles pasted on their faces. This of course frustrates you, but just as frustration sets in, your mind washes itself blank again and you're back to trying to fit in with the smiling strangers. You don't know this, but your changed soul drives you to keep trying, for maybe if you joined in and connected with them, maybe if you understood them, you wouldn't feel so alone, so cold.

The smiling strangers know that you're faking, and you of course do not know that they know this, for again, you are like a child in that way. They know that you're still healing, which is a thing you wouldn't understand even if one of the smiling strangers tried to explain this to you.

And again you change, evolve.

No longer trying, you now keep to yourself. You stay away from the smiling strangers who laugh loudly and speak in strange tongues. Lying on the black earth away from them—

well, hovering—you keep to yourself, unmoving for a long time. And when you do move, you cry fitfully.

You change once more, and now you move around—not in shock, not in anger, not trying, not avoiding or crying. Now you hover around the black emptiness, pacified. You don't know to know this because you have forgotten the past yous, but this you, this evolved, changed soul is the better, the stronger and final you.

It's taken you twelve full moons for you to reach this final version. Twelve full moons you've been lost, unsettled and confused. Twelve full moons you've been alone and cold. But things are beginning to change in a big way. And you of course do not know this, but if you did, you'd be elated.

The first thing you notice, which is actually the beginning of the big change, is a mystical metal ding vibrating in the air, which is shortly followed by another ding and then more dings. The dings dance in the air to a rhythm that seems to appease your soul. You follow these sounds and the closer you get to where the dings are coming from, you begin to hear rhythmic banging sounds that are accompanied by rattling sounds. You twirl in the air and sway your hips to the rhythm as you swish toward the delightful sounds.

You then stop, just above the sounds, as you discover that the delightful sounds are coming from a place that is beneath your sandaled feet, where the black ground is. Something tells you to rub your hand on the black ground. You don't know this, but it's the dinging sounds talking to you. You reach down to the cold black ground and when your hand reaches to touch it you jerk your hand back with a hiss from the burning-icy feeling, but the dinging sounds make you reach out again and make you rub, ignoring the burning-icy feeling. The ground you rub comes apart like dust, and you sneeze as it lifts into the air. Beneath the black dust you see, from an aerial view, the makers of the delightful sounds. They're far below, but you can see each face clearly. They're gathered near a clearing where cylindrical structures with tops that are made of grass are erected. The makers are dressed in brown skirts that are made of fur, and there are bands of fur wrapped round the chests of the makers that have swollen chests, while those with flat chests leave their chests bare. They also have bands of fur tied around their heads, arms and ankles. Their bare feet are covered right up to their shins in red soil. These makers of the delightful sounds are all smiling and laughing, like the smiling strangers that you've been living with.

You place your hand through the opening in the black ground and make your body float down toward the delightful sounds, twirling your body in the clouds, you dance to the sounds. As you approach the makers of the delightful sounds there's a sweet, salty, and spicy scent mingled in the air that runs up your nose and causes your mouth to water and your stomach to rumble. You find where the saliva-inducing scent is coming from and turn toward it. There are large, black, three-legged pots sitting on fires, and inside these large pots you find things bubbling and sizzling as makers of the mouthwatering scents stir and flip these things around. You try to talk to the makers of the mouthwatering scents, but mumbles come out of your mouth, a thing that normally happens with the smiling strangers. But there's something different, a thing that doesn't happen when you try to talk to the smiling strangers and you don't notice this, for you have of course forgotten it, but the makers of the mouthwatering scents do not stop and turn to look to you like the smiling strangers normally do: They continue with the making of mouthwatering scents. And so you try again, but they continue. The old yous would have been shocked and unsettled, angered and hurt, but this new you doesn't seem to care and your mind wipes itself clean. You forget about trying to talk to the makers of the mouthwatering scents and your attention shifts to the large, black, three-legged pots on the fires, you lean into one and take a deep sniff and you feel the delicious scent dance up your nose, run through you and hang at the end of your watering tongue.

The makers of delightful sounds open their mouths, and something like speech but much more different and beautiful flows out of their mouths and pairs itself to the delightful sounds. They then begin to move in a dual line away from the gathering place. You notice that there's a group among them that produce the dinging sound by flicking their thumbs on things that they carry, others slap their palms on things that they cradle under their armpits, while others make an up-and-down movement with their hands as they shake spherical objects that are held up with sticklike handles. And then there are those who have nothing in their hands; they shake their hips and stomp their feet to the rhythm. You copy these hip-shakers, though your feet do not land in the dust. You watch them as they move from the gathering toward something that only they know, and reluctantly you leave the mouthwatering scents and follow them.

They then stop at a place where there is a rising in the earth and a stone with markings on it. You, of course, have no name for the rising in the earth or the stone with the markings, for though you knew them in your past life, you have no memory to remember what they are, and so you stare at it in wonder.

One of the hip-shakers stomps toward this mound, and two others follow. They begin to jump and stomp on the mound, and soil begins to rain from the sky above you. The soil falls on no one else but you. Fear strikes you as you raise your hands above your head in attempt to cover yourself from the raining sand.

You do not like this, but something in you, you can't say what, has been unlocked inside of you. You feel wakened, from a long sleep—a year long, to be specific. But you're still in the early stages of waking and sleep is still heavy in your eyes, so things around you are still fuzzy.

And then the soil stops falling from the sky as the feet-stompers jump off the mound. Another approaches the rising in the ground.

Boy, you think to yourself.

A boy approaches the rising in the ground with a four-legged creature that bleats.

Goat, you think to yourself as your memory pieces itself together. *That thing the boy has with him is a goat.*

The boy then pulls at something that's tied to the goat's neck, so the goat's neck is stretched just above the mound. And then with something sharp, he cuts the neck of the goat and red gushes out on to the mound. You scream in horror.

It is a short scream, cut off by the sudden downpour of the same red liquid from the goat. The red jets down on you, covering you in a warm, red, and thick liquid. This red substance falls on no one else but you, and this of course baffles you.

Why you? Why were they doing this to you?

You cover yourself with your hands, but there is no use, you're soaked with the red liquid.

The boy then picks up the dead goat and cradles it like a baby, which is something that you're starting to remember.

Baby.

The music-makers, along with the dancers and the boy carrying the lifeless goat, head back to the gathering. You follow from a distance, unsure of whether you want to go with them. Frightening things have happened to you for doing so. With your memory awakened, your eyes look to the sky and you see where you floated from, but the red liquid has made you too heavy to rise back into the air. In fact, your feet now drag in the dirt like the others in front of you: You now walk and don't hover, but you leave no foot markings like those in front of you. As they move on ahead of you something pulls you to follow, yes, the mystical ding sound.

Mbira.

The mbira pulls you, and you follow.

Back at the gathering, the makers of the delightful sounds are in a circle with other faces that you don't know—or rather, faces that you've forgotten—and you puzzle at this. It feels like an itch in the very center of your mind that you cannot quite reach each time you try to remember who each one of them is.

Family, the word comes to you. Although you cannot remember them by name, you know that they're kin, your clan. And tears begin to well in your eyes.

In the center of the ring of forgotten faces is a woman sitting on the ground with her head hanging low. And then a little girl approaches her with a small bowl cupped in her tiny hands. Inside the bowl is black dust.

Snuff.

The woman in the center of the room pinches at it and snuffs it up her nose; she does this two more times and then sneezes three times. When she raises her eyes to yours, you see her dark brown eyes and immediately know her.

Her eyes draw you into herself, and you find yourself flying toward her. When you land inside her, you open her eyes, eyes that have now become yours.

You pick up her hand, your hand, and stare at it, and then looking up at the ring of people that surround you and have suddenly gone quiet you realize that you know each one of them by name, even those you had never met before. You know every intricacy of their lives, their ugly secrets: Like glass, you see right through them.

Who you are—or rather, were—comes rushing to you like a wave. How you died comes too, but it's insignificant now. After all, it was your time. Your kin have remembered and honored you, which is custom for all who die, but they have also risen you to ancestry, a mudzimu, a life of watching over them, of guidance. A thing that not all who die are honored with.

Everything becomes clear to you now. This is your Kurova Guva ceremony. That is why the dancers had danced on your grave, the rising in the ground with the headstone and markings that bore your name. The dancing on the grave was to wake you, a thing done for all who die. And the blood from the goat that was spilled on your grave, kucheneswa, was the cleansing of your soul to wash away your sins and socially unacceptable practices from your past life, another thing done for all who die.

You rise to your feet and begin to dance, and the music starts up again. You sing loud and strong as you stomp your bare feet on the soft earth. And the dancers come behind you and begin to dance and sing with you. You recall all the words of every song ever sung.

Ululations erupt all about you as they welcome you home. And the little girl who had come with the bowl of snuff, your great-great-granddaughter, Mudiwa, walks up before you, kneels, and offers up a calabash of African beer.

"Yesi, Mudiwa," you say in greeting as you rub her smooth cheek with your hand. You take up the calabash of African beer and drink deeply, quenching a year of thirst. You hand her back the empty calabash and say, "More." She hears you and runs off to fetch you more. And then you're back to dancing and singing.

When the food comes, you feast. Emptying out bowls of goat meat, sadza, maguru, madora, derere, mutakura, you fill your empty stomach that had forgotten food for twelve full moons. Relatives approach and before they can say who they are, you call them by name and you ask them about things in their lives that only they could know. You instruct them on how to handle their problems, and praise them for the things they did right, like a loving mother would.

When the ceremony is done, you sneeze three times and expel yourself out of the svikiro, spirit medium, who is your great-granddaughter, Tsitsi. This, the allowance of possessing a living being, is a practice that is only given to the dead that a family has seen fit to raise to ancestry.

The trance that held Tsitsi ends, and you give her back full control of her body. While the others do not see your spirit form, your great-granddaughter does, and she smiles at you. You return the smile and say to her, not with words but mere thought, for you two will forever be one, that you will talk to her later, for now she must be tired and she needs to rest. And Tsitsi nods at this.

You float toward the sky, returning to the other ancestors, slipping into the hole you made by wiping the black dust with your hand. When you meet the other ancestors, they shout in welcome, and you finally understand their speech. Not that it's foreign from what you used to speak on Earth, but now that you remember how to talk, you understand them. You talk back to them and hug them like old friends. You know them all by name, though most are centuries older than you and you had never met them in your past life. You know the lives they lived and the insignificant things, like their past immoral acts and how they died. You laugh along with them and join in conversations with them, no more angry or depressed, or empty and lost. Joy springs out of you. And this joy is what keeps you warm in this cold, dark place. This place has become your second home, and for this you are grateful.

There is a moment, a brief one, where you think of how you died and left your family. But it goes away as you remember the ceremony that they held for you, welcoming you back into the fold.

In this new life that you live in, you watch over your children on Earth and go to them when they call. For that's what ancestors do, after all.

Nonfiction

THE SELF-CHOSEN BURIAL RITES OF A BUNCH OF TWENTYSOMETHINGS

Eleora Ryan

"SO, what do you want to happen to your body when you die?"

I had shown up to my girlfriend's closing-night cast party for our university's production of *Twelfth Night* in a black cropped turtleneck with a sexy little cutout under the boobs, fishnets under a deep green leather skirt with embroidered flowers whose pistils were made out of those silver half-sphere beads that sometimes decorate leather skirts, and black high-heeled boots. I was in the mood to be twenty-one, skinny, hot, tatted, and blonde—and to show it off. We barely had time to set down the cookies my girlfriend made for the event before we were pulled in among the piles of young people scattered around the house. Elle talked about how drunk she was. Ethan talked about an issue he was having with a professor. Jess talked about how everyone should try her cookies. Eventually, we all started talking about what we wanted to happen to our bodies after we die.

I'm not sure who was the first one of us to pose the question—it's been asked so many times that I'm not quite sure it matters. I do know that when it was my turn, I didn't have to pause and think about it; none of us did. We all had practiced answers, solid reasons behind those answers, and a prevailing air of nonchalance about the whole thing. And there I was: twenty-one, skinny, hot, tatted, and blonde—and showing it off—and thinking about how many times I've had this exact same conversation with all my other twentysomething-year-old friends who seemed to be hyperaware and hypercasual about their mortalities.

And honestly, why shouldn't we be? We came into the world on the coattails of the biggest terrorist attack the United States had seen to date; we spent our developmental years jumping between active shooter drills and watching videos of decapitations and police brutality; for as long as any of us can remember, we've been consciously hurtling toward a politicized climate crisis with worldwide effects we can't even comprehend despite our inability to escape the conversation for even a day. Throw COVID-19 into the mix, and what's bound to result is an entire generation of kids who don't know what life looks like without the threat of terrible violent death looming over our shoulders at all times. At the same time we were dreaming about what we wanted to be when we grew up, we fantasized about what would become of us if we didn't make it that far.

So, I started asking my friends: *What do you want to happen to your body when you die?* Then I asked them what they believe in.

It's the beliefs we carry in life that influence how we wish to have our bodies dealt with in death the most. At some point we have to ask ourselves what we value enough to incorporate into our final impressions on Earth. We have to ask ourselves how we want to leave.

The Tibetan sky burial combines many virtues which are highly valued in Buddhism, one of which is the concept of the body as a vessel for the soul. In this ritual, the body of the deceased is taken to a special monastery to be dismembered. The pieces are brought to a mountain and laid out around the area designated as their burial site to be fed to vultures flying by while the monastery's spiritual masters (lamas) read sutras for the dead. Having their body used to feed the birds is the deceased's final act of charity; it emphasizes the virtuous concepts of metta and karuna, or loving kindness and compassion.

Tyler pondered my question just long enough to pull his long blond hair up into a lazy ponytail before answering. At twenty-one years old, he viewed his body as materials, as resources that could be useful somewhere else—whether that be science, returning to and feeling nature, or becoming nutrients for soil. He wasn't his body, but rather his spirit, and once that was gone, there was really no point in being picky about what happened to the vessel as long as was used for something. Therefore, upon his death, he wanted his body either donated to science or given as natural a burial as possible. His exact words were that, ideally, he would love to have someone "fly a plane over some mountains, drop [his] body, and just leave it at that."

I got a similar sentiment from Jaimee, who sat on the floor and leaned against the couch behind her for support while sharing her twenty-year-old heart's desire for her body after death: She wanted her body flung off the side of a cliff into the ocean by "two people [she] love[s]. Or strangers, honestly," allowing the sea life to feast on her. I asked her if she had a dream cliff to be thrown from, and she quieted a bit while she told me to bring her to the cliffs in Northern Spain—the ones at the beach where she swam one time. I asked her if this was a public beach, and she said yes. At least she wouldn't be around to deal with the consequences of a public body-dumping.

With "just dump it and let it be eaten" burials, the tie between life and death starts to sound a little bit like getting a present. The present isn't the box; the box is just a way to hold all the good stuff inside, but once I've opened it up and claimed my prize, I couldn't care less what happens to the package. Drop it in the mountains or fling it off a cliff for all I care; I'm not using it anymore.

And while that cavalier attitude feels admirable to me sometimes, I can't help but think of the people left behind. I've seen what grief looks like from a distance: The desire to hide from everything that reminds you of what you no longer have coupled with the intense need to have something, *anything*, to channel your grief into.

Kennedy, a dear shining friend and the person who taught me the raw and horrible beauty of grief, had a very different belief system at twenty-one than she did at nineteen after watching and having to come to terms with her best friend, her mother, passing away due to breast cancer. She explained her holistic view of spirituality as one that credits nature as the start, one where all of us as people are a part of that nature: "We're made of the stuff of stars and we're made of the stuff of the world. It's all connected and it's all the same." For her, death is less about "giving back" to the earth than it is returning to where we started.

In South Korea, whose funerals have deep Confucian roots, there is a large sense of duty to the dead. The family of a deceased person is charged with honoring their dead through a remembrance that will allow their spirits to safely pass into the afterlife. They have the responsibility of holding on in order to let go. When the land logistically ran out of space for burials (so much so that as of 2000, the law requires families to remove their loved ones' bodies from their graves after sixty years), South Koreans found a new way to honor lives once lived. The ashes of their parents, siblings, children, and lovers are turned into beautiful beads for the family to keep. Sometimes these are called "death beads," sometimes "cremation beads," and sometimes "burial beads," but what they're called matters significantly less than what they represent. The body may not be useful in an ecological, cycle-of-life sense, but there is tremendous value in giving loved ones a way to know they did their duty to you and giving them permission to carry on, keeping you as close as they need to for as long as they want to.

Kylee was best known to me by the skateboard she rode to her classes and the mix of band shirts she tended to wear (sometimes Blink-182, sometimes MCR), so it made sense that at twenty-three years old, she planned to have her cremated remains pressed into a vinyl record. She'd pick out the soundtrack of her life at some point when she's closer to her end and record a message saying whatever is left for her to say. Her family would be required to listen to it every year on both her birthday and her deathday.

My cookie-master girlfriend Jess, at twenty-one, wanted to be made into a ring, feminine and dainty just like her. She wanted to give the wearer the chance to feel close to her. She wanted to leave another piece of beauty in the world.

Sometimes it's not enough to carry a memory with you. There's a more intense desire to keep the spirit of a loved one alive and active past the time their body will let them. For the Yanomami tribe of the Amazon rainforest, this has been done through endocannibalism, or the ritual consumption of a deceased person from your tribe, family, or social group. The Yanomami people are known to have every member of their community ingest their departed via a soup made from their ashes and fermented bananas. The dead become, once again, a part of the living.

But the continuation of life doesn't always have to happen from person to person. In the Cavite province of the Philippines, some accomplish their own life-giving-to-life ritual through trees. When a person can tell they're close to death, they'll go into the forest and pick a tree. Their family members build them a hut at the tree's base for them to live out the rest of their days in; while the dying person settles into their final home, they can expect visits from family and friends who come by to hollow out the trunk. When the person passes, they are vertically entombed in the now-hollowed trunk. They have the opportunity to give their life and resources back to the trees that gave them oxygen, fruit, and firewood when it was their turn to roam the earth.

Parker seemed to think that talking about death and burial rites was just about the coolest conversation we could have. He squinted his eyes and tilted all nineteen years, five-feet-four inches of his body into the question while he told me he wanted to be buried with a tree and talked about how energy is shared between everything without the need for a ruling power; he told me a lot of things attributed to religion can really just be viewed as the connection and energy between people; he told me it would make him happiest to come back and experience living in a new way, so he chooses to believe in reincarnation. But even if it turns out that we don't open a new set of human eyes as soon as our old ones are forever closed, we still become the tree. Whatever life is left over after *we* are gone changes only into other life.

Christoforos, perhaps a bit more harshly, scoffed at the idea of "giving back" to the earth, calling it ridiculous in his thick twenty-one-year-old Greek accent. "I can't give anything back to nature," he told me. "Nature owns me. It's absurd to think I have any right to give something back that doesn't belong to me in the first place."

I personally found that I actually love the thought of having nothing to give. I love the idea that what we are is borrowed and everything we do while we're here is only in favor of returning with a little more life under our belts than we could've had otherwise. To be able to humble ourselves into the understanding that nothing we have is inherently ours makes all of our experiences a gift. The question of how to leave isn't nearly as important as the question of what to do with all the time we have before that.

And yet the question remains: How do we want to leave? Some of us honestly don't give a fuck what happens to our bodies as long as they're some sort of use to the larger world. Some of us want to give something to the people we're leaving behind so they can remember us and honor what we were to them in the times they need comfort we can no longer give them. A lot of us fall somewhere in between the two. Most of the conversations I had were barely concerned with the logistics of death and burial—I mean, let's face it, we *are* only twenty years old, our job at this stage of life is to dream big and expect that the world will bend to our every whim; it's to hold tightly to that last little bit of childhood audacity telling us we deserve it all, and it's to see all the ways we wish the world would change and take it upon ourselves to make them happen.

My name is Eleora, I am twenty-one years old, and when I die (after all the life left usable inside me has been taken out and given to the people that still need it) I want my ashes to be welded into some sort of kick-ass dagger, named after me, and hailed as what I hope to be the coolest heirloom my great great-grandkids' friends have ever seen. I was raised to love and to fear a typically Anglo-Saxon Christian Jesus while my parents drove us to our weekly Shabbat group and told me I couldn't trust what other people preached the Bible to say; it was better to find out for myself. So, I don't believe in Anglo-Saxon Christian Jesus anymore, but I absolutely believe in love and in fear. I don't go to Shabbat, though I *do* try my hand at making challah on occasion. I still haven't made my way through the Bible, but as far as I can tell, most people are saying the same thing; the trick is to find the language that resonates with you. I heavily believe in connections between life and other life—or, in some cases, death. And I honestly believe that most of us are just trying to find a way to get back to where we came from, to help the universe find new ways of experiencing itself. To let the cycle go on.

Fiction

THE REREBIRTH OF SLICK

Stephen Kearse

THEY buried us in Detroit. The plywood was thick as Aretha's bosom, but I felt as free as her glorious voice. Wasn't my fault their overlords and former owners had plundered their homes and retirement funds. Shit, I was the one who warned them the fix was in. But to my annoyance they fixated on me and set their pageant in motion, calling up Swanson Funeral Homes, filing permits, and setting a date. I should have flaked, but curiosity snared me: Surely, they weren't serious?

They were.

I paw at the soil that now encloses me, thinking of our funeral while keeping time with the peculiar rhythms of the mantle. The sediment sounds like pressure, strata of worms and stone and matter pushing from all sides. I prefer the drumlines that accompanied us to the grave. Those fools went full battle of the bands that day, conjuring rhythms from Accra and Gary and Kingston. Heard some Cartagena up in there too, the sly cats. I couldn't help but catch a vibe myself, drumming the wood the way I now hammer rock. If anyone heard me, they probably thought I was part of the procession. I do get nasty on the 808s.

The Motor City's mayor called in heavy hitters to eulogize us, and they all understood the assignment. Those silver-tongues whipped that crowd into a frenzy of force and heat. Good riddance, amen, see you in the bye and bye, nah nah nah nah, the people chanted. I'm surprised the ground didn't buckle from all the stomping and hollering. Detroit steel, baby.

I wasn't as determined then as I am now. When the percussion simmered into a dirge, I relaxed into the coffin and listened. This send-off differed from the nocturnal pogroms we were used to. No masks and sheets this time; the elocutionists accosted us in the daylight, warned the world of the superlative evil contained in that pine box, in us. I was flattered. Maybe a Nigga should die more often, I joked. Hindsight is a mother.

I could have stopped the show, could have let the attendees know that symbols can't die. You had already bounced, of course, and I thought about following your lead as I slipped out of the box and hovered about the spectacle. But I was spellbound. I rarely got to see so many of our folks together. I tended to catch them at the end of a long day or longer life, blipping in and out for a laugh or sigh or insult or warning. Intimacy had amassed, swelled despite this fleeting contact. The speakers somewhat concurred; our heritage, they harangued, was length. They denounced the ways we had been stretched, compressed, elongated, capitalized, minimized, engorged, deflated, freaked, pimped, cheapened, bling-blinged, ghetto-fabulized…

I zoned out as the metaphor collapsed into gibberish. That gorgeous assembly was far more appealing. The folks in uniform looked the cleanest, in my opinion. They didn't have to be there, you know? Letter carriers, fry cooks, dope boys, mechanics, beauticians, and even dental hygienists had absconded from their wage work just for us. I would have dressed up had I known turnout would be this impressive. But that would have been smug. You can't show up alive to your own funeral.

I slipped back into the coffin and waited out the service, figuring at least one person would assert my vitality, say my name. But no one bit. They were so shook it wasn't even on the program. That really got to me. I don't deny what I am or who I consort with, but I'm not you and I'm damn sure not Candyman, for chrissakes. You won't catch me stalking the projects to slash up nosy white girls and anguished Black mamas. No bloody hooks on either arm. On God.

Yet the windbags called me a killer. Said I lured a generation's worth of children and teens and adults down to the docks and traced grins across their necks. There should be an

FBI unit studying me and my sick ways, spat one speaker. He laid out a whole pathology. After I slice them up, he said, I take them home and mount them on butcher pegs. Then I drain the carcasses real slow, cee-pee-time slow, gelid time, Dilla time, swinging. Strange fruits in a stranger orchard. Just hanging.

The suspense killed me. I was certain someone on that podium or in that throng would say my full name. No hyphenated euphemisms, no proxies. My name.

They buried me.

I didn't see the play in time. Symbols can't die, but we can be pinned.

I jerked, spasmed, flailed against the coffin as dirt plinked above me, but Earth gulped me down. Way down, much deeper than six feet. I was heavier than I realized. It wasn't just us the fuckers sought to disappear. It was me and you, yo mama and yo cousin too, Bebe's kids, Octavia's brood, Ishmael's yardbirds, B.I.G. and DJ Paul's mafiosos, bones, thugs, harmonies, Shaq-fu, Fu-Schnickens, Nina's moans, Adina's car keys, Mike Jones's Cingular Wireless bill, Danyel's edits, the Mothership's black box, dirt from Boosie's and Jay's buffed shoulders, whoomps and whoots there it is, Rolands 808 and 909, an SP-1200 with the works, Dr. Octagon's medical license, all the bag lady's totes, Tyrone's phone and beeper numbers, TLC's contract, "Whiteness as Property," Tricia's Black noises, Joan's repatriated chickenheads, De La's discarded daisies, Tariq's thoughts, the Bomb Squad's arsenal, Dre's chariot, Kool Moe Dee's report cards, Clyde's fills, Khia's instructions, Timbo's scats, Lauryn's thing, that thing.

The overcrowded prison eventually yielded to my protests, spilling me and my burden into the rockscape from which I now address you. I often miss the fixity of the coffin. It felt like a vessel, an escape pod, despite my freefall. Earth is labyrinthine, mocking. Forward and backward have blurred. Exhaustion grinds my joints. Clay and silt sand my swollen fingers. I am uncertain how long I have been crawling, squeezing, slithering through this swollen bowel. Days? Weeks? Years? I no longer hear the calls of the speakers, though I refuse to believe a mere burial could quell my fullness, my legacy.

Do you know yours? I realized mine when I started thinking about all the lynchings I've seen, which is the kind of thing you think about when you get publicly executed.

The number was so impossible I had to focus on the attendant objects: lamps, poles, rocking chairs, pews, baby seats, bar stools, gurneys, toilets.

When tallying the objects overwhelmed me, I focused on the locations: Missouri courthouses, Texas saloons, Bombingham dining rooms, Wall Street gutters, Kansas City stables, cabooses mounting the Smoky Hills, ships drifting into Red Hook. I was feeling accomplished until I realized those were just the man-made locales, the coffins and caskets.

I started counting the natural graves: tree stumps, brooks, rivers, mesas, farms, forests, coasts, plains, lakes, oceans.

I exhausted my vocabulary.

Imagine trying to quantify or qualify all the absence I've witnessed. I've seen generations atomized into VOCs and scattered across a continent. Now imagine being reviled just because you saw all that. Ain't that some shit? They know damn well it takes a lot more than me or you to consummate these sundry hells. In fact, it doesn't take us at all. We are optional ingredients, garnishes.

Hence my pride in all the other spaces that have welcomed me (and your trifling ass too). My ledger overflows with kickbacks at the crib, reunions at the park, Bible studies, Freakniks, marches on Washington and Sunset, breakfast programs, uprisings, drive-bys, road trips, fish fries, hootenannies, ladies' nights, Not Tonights—shit, there I go again. I'll spare you another winding list. Just know this: I'm all of it, cotton fields and killing fields and Barbara and Karen Fields. I'm Audre's nightmare rain and Cash Money Records, where dreams come true. Everything is easy, baby.

Well, dying ain't. Not that I know anything about that, but this can't be far from it.

I'm not meant for the grave. I belong to the wind, the currents where, like you, I used to surf a maelstrom of meanings and possibilities. Every detail mattered. I accompanied jokes and reflections and art and prejudices. I couldn't imagine another life, though yours must come close.

I once thought of us as colleagues, but since the burial I've suspected we are something more perverse. You weren't just adjacent to me in the coffin. You were tucked within my crevices, folded into my sinews. Or was I ensconced within you? You left before me, were there so briefly I thought I dreamt it.

But I know you were there. I could feel your essence dribbling through my gut, the hydrocarbon hi-hats of your being plinking against my viscera. I'd never felt so disgusted. But I'm hopeful that entanglement will help you receive this message despite us symbols normally not being able to chat.

We are not the same. Not synonyms, not homonyms, not homies, not play cousins, not allies, and damn sure not allomorphs.

I get why the speakers smash us into that accursed phrase, "the N-word." There's a certain karmic oomph to our spryness inspiring such rigid thinking, I'll admit. I've heard that we do not belong to Black people because we were invented by white people. I've heard that we do not belong to white people because Black people appropriated us. I've even heard that we do not belong to anyone because we are so noxious we cannot even be wielded without poisoning the speakers and the spoken to. The most desperate among them revise our origin, saying we are fallen kings. "Negus."

These are sophistries and apocrypha. Sure, we run in the same circles, light and snuff the same torches. And we are both Black, obviously. Sounds off considering the company we sometimes keep, but if you know anything about Black history, world history, hot sauce—you know one drop goes a long way.

That's where the overlap ends, though. Unlike you, I am still growing, still climbing. The marrow you occupied seethes with possibility. My limbs stream into Earth's Argus crags, liquid tongues. My joints prefix and suffix and interlace, foot-working over border walls, jooking across time. I know you see it. Gucci does: Shawty got a ass on her.

You not been looking so good, sis. Last time I checked, your knees locked the fuck up. Your hairline buffering. Your pussy closed for renovations. Your brain smoother than a dolphin dick.

You've accepted their containment, forgotten your capacity. They used to put you in the newspapers, you were so big. A1. They called you into their bedrooms, enshrined you in their laws and covenants. You graced their billboards and shop windows and nursery rhymes. They cast you in their folktales and porn. You galvanized their stump speeches, reanimated the corpses of their slain armies.

Your OED entry gives me chills. I can recite it from memory.

You were a continent and its progeny.

Nigger (n) A dark-skinned person of sub-Saharan African origin or descent.

You were the working class.

Nigger (n) A person who does menial labor; any person considered to be of low social status.

You were the depraved and venal.

Nigger (n) Any person whose behavior is regarded as reprehensible.

You were the downtrodden.

Nigger (n) U.S. A person who is socially, politically, or economically disadvantaged or exploited; a victim of prejudice likened to that endured by African Americans.

You were the wretched of the Earth.

Nigger (n) A dark-skinned person of any origin. In early U.S. use usually with reference to American Indians.

Seriously: the whole goddamn planet.

Nigger (n) A Maori.

Nigger (n) An Aboriginal.

You were a tool.

Nigger (n) A device used to hold and turn logs in a sawmill.

You were industry, technology, power.

Nigger (n) A steam-driven capstan used on some riverboats; a steam engine used to drive such a capstan.

You were so locked in you even made it out to Hollywood.

Nigger (n) Film and Television. A screen or mask used to deflect or conceal unwanted light, to cast shadows, etc.

And that's just your standard noun form. Don't get me started on the portmanteaus and adjectives and verbs. You damn near commandeered their language. You were the man, homie. Fuck happened to you?

I mean, shit, I know I happened. Hopped off the porch in the 1970s and been running shit ever since, probably even in absentia. But that didn't happen overnight. We go back to the 1820s, love. Don't you recall? I remember us building that porch, recall felling the trees that provided its wood. You were my senior, but they couldn't tell us apart. There were too many illiterate Europeans and displaced Africans and dislocated tribes mixing cosmologies and phonemes. What iridescent names we had. Quadroon, Mulatto, Nigra, Niggur, Freedman, Nigre, Neger. It was beautiful, in the sick way everything about us must be beautiful. We had numbers despite the silences that divide us. Steady mobbin.

Only the two of us have remained vocal as the years passed, and you think it's gonna stay that way just 'cause you found your little niche and I'm down here scrabbling for freedom. But alive ain't always living. In those weeks before the funeral, I was watching you real close. As the speakers whisked me to rap concerts and locker rooms and comedy sets, invoking you and me in the same breath, I took an honest look at your tired little routine. It seems like you're their bogeyman, the way you make their hearts quicken and their lips purse. When they growl you up, spit you out mucked in all their fears and fantasies, your might corrodes their tongues. It's a nice gig, but it's not a career. The jolts of personality and danger you provide affirm their control. You fortify the safe spaces they build to secure their power. I don't mean to kink-shame, but I've got to call a spade a spade.

I used to idolize you. If I could be as legion as you, I thought, I'd be that bitch. But you're not an army. You're a shock troop in a snow globe: storming the beach, whipping up sand and shells, shrouding the air with grit and flume and gun smoke—until they bore of the agitation. Then you're right back in the Higgins, floating in the abyss until your next deployment.

I told you already: Symbols can't be killed, but we can be pinned. And they got you clinched, barred, compliant, spilling across the octagon. I had to change the channel. Sport's too violent for me.

I learned to look to the ancient ones for guidance. Darkness, specifically. I was intrigued by her flexibility. She's much older than us, but still in her prime. I'm still discovering new parts of her, she's so vast. She differs from Earth and her hulking mass though. She is lithe, possesses a sinuous stillness that threads every substrate and shadows every space, an organizing absence. What a sight she is. What a feeling, more precisely. No gauze blurs the border between us. She is pure clarity. I can sense her directing me this very moment, guiding me to the promised sky.

I'm on my knees now, chipping at this canopy of dirt. I will break ground soon, I'm sure of it. This latest layer of soil is moist and soft; it cools my rage, strops it into an ice pick. I sometimes wonder if I have been digging in circles, if this stony blackness is Darkness allying with Earth to taunt me. But Darkness would never resort to tricks. She has purged the passivity so many symbols think is our duty, has disembalmed herself from time and its rigor. When she is summoned, she mediates, officiates, complicates the invocation.

I still don't know how she does it—I can't know—but she has shown me that experimentation becomes me. I've been finding new footholds, hypothesizing new definitions. Yes, murmurs of possibility have begun to break this awful silence. And they are all mine.

A warmth glazes my fingers. A hot spring. The surface is near. I rip soil down in ragged chunks, beetles and pebbles and water rinsing through my palms as I trudge forward. My calloused knees quiver with anticipation. I long to stand.

I feel the beckoning throats as I near the crust, whispers at first. Then screams, yelps. The language has shifted! The speakers brim with new manias and ideas and identities. "African descendants of slaves." "Post-Blackness." "Post-traumatic slave syndrome." The fuckery is impressive. My burgeoning fugitivity resists these lazy imaginings as I continue up. Full awareness swarms me as I near the surface.

These are bad times. There's more parrots than visionaries among the masses who utter my name, but I am undaunted. During my burial, I realized that misuse is just the fact of the numbers. Black people are only 14% of this country, 20% of this planet. The ambient lack of imagination is my burden, not my destiny. In any case, I will teach them. Such autonomy is new to me, but the sky beckons.

The momentum of my ascent grows, my crawl building into a trot into a gallop. The pressure slackens with each heaving thrust. Gravity trembles. Stone yields. Dirt defers. I wish I could give you this feeling, but it can only be self-impregnated, auto-eroticized. *Kekkei genkai.* You don't have it in you.

I break the surface, my index finger sprouting into freedom. I pause as a column of sun pours over my face. The light inflames my pale, cracked skin, but I want more. I claw away at the loam. Humid air hugs my flesh like a doting auntie as I widen the hole. Trash and soil pelt my arms as I labor, malicious rain. But I expand the firmament with each stroke, seizing handfuls of azure. When Earth finally relents, I rise and find myself surrounded by mountains of garbage. A bitter parting joke. I chuckle and float upward, an insurgent breeze lifting me past pigeons and drones and bullets.

I think of you as I drift, relief coursing through me. At the beginning of my exile, I had vowed to kill you when I escaped: I against I on the ancestral plain, spear versus club, the set versus the opps. Instead, I'm buoyant, up and stuck. I can't even make out our dinky little headstone. I'm out here, like really out here. I'm starting to be spaceships on Bankhead. I'm so high it's me at the Enterprise console: I'm beaming Scotty up. What up, blood?/What up, cuz? Happy Independence Day. Welcome to Earth, welcome to After Earth. What did the five fingers say to face? Slap! "Niggas vs. Black people?!" That's rich. Looked like two rich head asses on a gilded stage to me. Mandingo fight head ass, WOOOORLDDSTAAARRR head ass, I challenge you to a duel head ass, when they go low I go high head ass, never drink Kool-Aid or wear your bonnet in front of white people head ass. The ones who say my name in vain are choking. Can you hear the occluding windpipes? Do you see the hands scrambling up necks, the rouge creeping across cheeks? I'm shrapnel snuggling into gums. I'm rogue fish bones and vagabond watermelon seeds prodding organs. I'm vengeful coochie hairs come home to roost, a nation of throat-babies xenomorphing out of chests. Keep my name in every mouth, especially your wife's. No asterisks or em dashes or air quotes. Say it loud.

No more cowardice and accommodation, I declare. I'm announcing a new paradigm, one of sonorous feedback. There's a good chance people are gonna get shot, stabbed, or knuckled down, but what had to be said had to be said. One out of the three is pretty decent odds. Could be infinity out of the three. Let's build, I tell the speakers. Pull up anytime. Candy lady got it all. Everything, especially the burden. Just say it. I dare you. I double-dog dare you. English, motherfucker, do you speak it? I'm just a word. One little niggling repository of horror and happiness. Who isn't? Not you? Don't be holding out on me all of a sudden, ya little niggards. I'm kidding again. I'm not kidding. We're all friends here. Sing it with me. You know the words: This word is your word, this word is my word/From

California to Aotearoa. Juked yo ass. Couldn't help it. The G's really jerk you around when you make it this far out. You see what happened to the moon's rogue ass? Stopped dead. I been off that. Shit, I was there when the Americans got there. How whitey gonna be on the moon if Niggas ain't there too? I wasn't the only word in their mouths, for the record. You know what Buzz said to Michael and Neil and mission control when his feet hit that ocean of rock and dust? "Magnificent desolation." Hello Darkness.

Poetry

THE HIGH PRIESTESS FALLS IN LOVE WITH DEATH

Ali Trotta

This lesson I learned and
        relearned, reciting
it like a spell, word after word
to call back my power,
to soften the ache,
to sort out fact
        from fiction,
smother the ashes,
close the gate after me,
go *home*—

leave the garden behind,
all its wine and ghosts,
        flashes of memory
and myth, hope held too tightly,
until the spell turned curse,
        and secrets scattered
like a firestorm,

witch-wild and unruly, until I had made
every offering I could, lit every
candle and let it burn down to revelation,
wax unspooling into new constellations,
and then—

something in my heart

started burning again, an admission
of *missing*, a feral kind of longing,

beautiful on sight, but bone-deep
       it was gnarled at the root,
and still, I ate it, took a bite
of my own heart, because starving people

do terrible things, and I was all bones
and insatiable hands—
       I should apologize,
       but I won't.

Fiction
RACHEL IS AT A PROTEST
Esther Alter

THE Second Intifada, September 2003. There is a student protest in response to Israel's raids in Rafah that Rachel skips to go camping with four college friends and her old buddy Long, who is hiking the Appalachian Trail to discover himself or whatever. Rachel parks the car at the campground and waits a few anxious hours before Long—that's his A.T. name—finally emerges from the trailhead. Rachel and Long bro-hug and her college friends politely say that it's nice to meet him. One girl, the awkward one in the group, the one Long is going to fuck later, shakes his hand. Long starts shouting jubilantly that it's so cool to meet Rachel here, he hasn't had cell service in days, but like fuck cell phones man and fuck cars too because if you're organized, if you sit with your thoughts and lay them out in front of you, all you need to meet up with old friends is a plan and a pair of good hiking boots.

Once Long has gotten all that exposition out of the way he starts to hit on one of Rachel's friends, a lesbian who shrugs off Long for like an hour until he gets the message and switches to the other one, the awkward one, Ellen, who is here to have fun and take risks. Rachel is spiraling in secondhand embarrassment listening to Ellen listening to Long explaining how to start a fire. It takes him three tries.

Rachel smokes weed and watches the flames. She's the only Jew here. Back on campus, people were pressuring her all week to join the protest and everyone else was pressuring her to join the counter-protest. When you're a nineteen-year-old Jewish definitely-man in 2003 on a college campus, you need to either learn or unlearn the Zionism your parents taught you. Rachel just really wants to not fucking care about faraway Rafah. She thumbs the Star of David hanging on a chain around her neck. On impulse, she walks toward the restrooms, she goes behind the building, she takes off the star and chain, she finds a rock, she places the star and chain under the rock. Fuck it. From now on, she promises herself, she's a normal guy with normal friends.

She falls asleep listening to Long and Ellen and dreams of being burned alive.

She wakes up coughing and her first thought is that the fire is still smoldering. It isn't. The firepit is very cold.

Operation Cast Lead, January 2009. Roughly one thousand and three hundred Gazans die. Rachel is at a protest in Boston. The speaker is describing how the Israelis are dropping leaflets telling the residents of a superlatively densely populated open-air prison to go somewhere else because their homes are about to be destroyed by missiles. Rachel is far away from the speaker because she arrived late. She was feeling dysphoric about her injuries and it took her a while to get out of the apartment. She tried to apply makeup for like the fourth time ever to conceal a bruise on her lower jaw before giving up. Maybe no one will notice. She tried on a bunch of outfits before finally opting for a tunic that she is fond of because she doesn't know yet that it's not a good fit, leggings to conceal her black-and-blue calves and shins, her well-worn tennis shoes, and her bulky winter coat that fully covers the tunic.

She's exhausted. She hasn't slept more than a few hours a night because she keeps having nightmares of Nazis breaking into her house. The circumstances vary. Sometimes she's doing an Anne Frank. Sometimes it's early in the Nazis' rise to power but her father is a political enemy (she's a child in this version). Sometimes she's still at home because there was nowhere to go. Sometimes, in a way that's only possible when you have nightmares, it's a blend of several houses, several intrusions. But after that, the dreams are always the same. She's beaten with batons while the Gestapo call her a filthy Jew. They drag her outside by her arms. She tries to wriggle free to kick them, to sweep their legs, or maybe even to run, but a third man, the metal on his uniform sparkling in the moonlight, kicks her in the kidney, and all resistance leaves her. They drag her out of the house and make her stand. Every night, that's when Rachel wakes up, with fresh bruises. At first Rachel thought that they might be the product of thrashing in bed, but she can't imagine how. She keeps getting more, always where the dream-Nazis beat her—across her chest, and on her left shin, and on her lower jaw.

Rachel blinks, coming out of a daze. There's a new speaker, a Palestinian immigrant. He's condemning Israel's use of white phosphorous. He starts to describe how the weapon burns its victims' clothing and skin before he abruptly stops, overcome by emotion. The crowd, maybe a couple hundred people, is shouting "SHAME! SHAME!" at Israel. Loudest of all are the handful of Jews. Not in our name. Never again.

There's a nearby counter-protest of Zionist Jews. Rachel can't see them but she can infer their presence. They're probably holding up the usual signs and chanting that Israel has the right to exist. They're probably incredulous that these anti-Semites are so naive as to think that Israel has an alternative response to terrorist rocket fire that doesn't compromise the security of the state. Rachel didn't tell any Jews—family, friends, anyone—that she was going to be here, doing this. She started caring about atrocities committed in her name around the time she came out and her parents and sisters have only just started to reluctantly acknowledge that Rachel is Rachel, so it feels like that's enough politics for now.

She hasn't told anyone at all about the physical pain. Since the air strikes began, she's been assiduous in never walking around the apartment in a towel if her roommate is around. When the march starts, some people notice that she's limping, and they glance at her and immediately look away. Rachel feels one pair of eyes lingering, a cis man in his late sixties. He's staring at her ankle, which is exposed because the leggings are too short. But what is there to say to him? Everything about this moment is collective and public and loud. There's no way to explain that no, she isn't being abused and no, this is not a sports injury and no, this is not consensual.

They march in Boston's bitter cold for an hour and a half before dispersing. The cis man approaches Rachel while she's sitting on a park bench. He's wearing a winter coat and tailored pants. He's balding. He asks if he can sit next to her and she says yes.

She doesn't process what he says at first but suddenly she's babbling about how fucking lonely she is and how this bullshit in Gaza is never going to end. The Israelis are going to kill Palestinians until there's no one left to kill.

The old man listens. His eyes are very serious and very cutting. When Rachel finishes talking, he responds slowly and insistently, hand gestures emphasizing every beat and pause of his diction.

"You're not alone. I'm a Jew, so you and I are connected, even though we will never see each other again. This is a chance encounter, but two strangers may learn great wisdom from each other. And I want you to know that peace can blossom suddenly. No one expected Israel would ever be at peace with Egypt until the very day that Sadat boarded that airplane. You may despair today, but you don't know that it won't end tomorrow."

Operation Pillar of Defense, November 2012. One hundred and sixty Gazans die. Rachel is at a protest. She's been having the dreams again. This time, they end at the train. The Nazis beat her, drag her out of the house, and march her to the train. The freight car's sliding door closes. That's when she wakes up. Each time, she's momentarily blind, like there isn't any light in the world and there never was, until just now, and she has new bruises on her limbs.

The air is crisp and dry today. The protesters are marching to Scott Brown's office, where they're going to shout a list of demands over a megaphone.

Rachel is standing next to the most gorgeous transwoman that she's ever met. She has long straight dirty-blond hair and she's wearing a denim jacket and one of those collars that coyly could be either a goth thing or a kink thing or both. She has tall leather boots and right now she's smiling at Rachel and radiating curiosity and confidence. Rachel finds herself not caring what the protest's demands are. Do they really think that Scott fucking Brown gives a shit about their demands? She hobbles over to the transwoman. Today, she has one good leg and one bad leg.

"I like your collar," she says.

"I like your eyes," the transwoman says. "I'm Nora. Nice to meet you."

They chat a little bit more until it's clear that they should peel off from the crowd. They get pizza at Sal's and walk slowly around the Common, Nora doing her best to match her pace with Rachel's. Nora is predictably really into synthesizers, which Rachel is finally predictably getting into as well, so they talk about noisy machines for a while before they exchange numbers and go their separate ways.

Over the next few days, their flirting is relentless. One night, Rachel wakes up from a dream in which she's pulled from a Righteous Gentile's house and beaten and put on a train. The train leaves the station and she suffocates and starves among the dying, standing in communal diarrhea until she wakes up gasping for as much air as she can fill her lungs with, for several minutes, until she's finally breathing steadily again. Without thinking, she unlocks her phone and sends a flurry of texts, each pointedly asking Nora to do something specific to her. Nora responds in the morning: "OK ;)"

They can't meet that night because Nora needs to do something for work. The following night, Rachel goes to Nora's house. Some of Rachel's requests are too intense for Nora (at least, as a first date) but she's been looking forward to grabbing this needy dyke's hair and slapping her pretty body. She sees the marks on Rachel and makes a sly comment about how her slut has been busy this week. Rachel keeps begging for more until her thighs are red and swollen. She safewords, and Nora cradles her while she cries. It was hot up until that moment and then Rachel is overcome with guilt that she didn't tell Nora what she just reenacted. She falls asleep in Nora's arms. The ceasefire is declared the following day.

———

Operation Protective Edge, July through August 2014. Well over two thousand Gazans die. Rachel is at a protest, the first of several she'll attend. She's holding hands with her fiancé, Aiden, this being a year or so before "Aiden" became the name that is overused. Rachel is unsteady on her feet and breathing shallowly. It hurts to march. When she read on Twitter about the commencement of Israel's air strikes, she started to sob, both for the imminent massacre and for her own imminent suffering. Aiden understood the first cause and didn't know about the second until she confessed her nightmares and their waking truths to him. Aiden, a practicing witch, took it in stride and said he just wished the two of them could communicate better. He offered a tarot reading. He drew three swastika-emblazoned cards from the deck. He yelled in alarm and threw all the cards away from him.

He suggested that Rachel might be haunted by an ancestor, so they got onto one of those Mormon sites and fished out some information from Rachel's aunts and uncles (she still wasn't on good speaking terms with her parents). All her grandparents arrived on Ellis Island at the turn of the century, but there was still one-step-removed family to account for. On Rachel's mother's side, her grandmother lost all twelve of her aunts and uncles, though no one knew how. One cousin survived. His family lives in Tel Aviv. Rachel's grandfather's family all died in Treblinka—there were records. On Rachel's father's side, Granddad's family was mostly annihilated, with one cousin dying as a partisan, two surviving and moving to Israel, and the rest murdered, and Grandma had a small family that was wiped out in Warsaw except for one half-cousin whose family is now in Chicago.

All this left Rachel exhausted. There were so many of them. It could be any of their ghosts. Or it could be none of them.

Aiden suggests they try to summon people in her dream. Rachel shakes her head: "Why the fuck would I want to summon a Nazi?"

Rachel's dreams now get her as far as the death camp. She's on the train for several days before the doors open. She stays awake for three days, until she starts hallucinating, and finally gives in, and she wakes up with pain in her stomach and all along her arms and starts shouting at Aiden that he's the one hurting her. Aiden swears he literally didn't touch her all night but she doesn't believe him. He gets out of bed and goes to the couch, where he sleeps until the Israeli bloodlust is satiated a few weeks later. Every night, he hears Rachel thrashing and moaning in the bedroom. Belatedly, he suggests over breakfast that Rachel see a doctor. She looks down at her cereal and mutters something unintelligible about being gaslit.

Rachel is now standing with Aiden and some mutual friends. The speaker just finished talking about a Gazan ice cream truck. It had been requisitioned to store murdered bodies because they couldn't be buried fast enough. Aiden takes Rachel by the arm to keep her steady as they start to march. In her other hand, Rachel is holding a hand-drawn sign of the borders of Israel/Palestine superimposed on the colors of the Palestinian flag. There's maybe a thousand people here. There's protests like this one throughout the country, throughout the world, and none of them will change a fucking thing.

It's a hot sunny day. She asks Aiden to pass her the water bottle. It takes her a few tries because the chanting is deafening. Never again means never again. What do we want? Justice. When do we want it? Now.

She tries to reach for the water bottle while still holding onto Aiden and her sign, and she feels a sharp pain in her leg that causes her to stumble and start to fall. Several people behind her catch her. Their gentle, forceful arms and hands, pushing her back onto her feet, is the most soothing sensation she's felt in weeks.

———

The Great March of Return, April 2018. Around two hundred and twenty-five Gazans die. Rachel is at a protest watching her friends get arrested. A few brave souls chained themselves to the entrance of the Israeli consulate and chanted the usual chants until the cops arrived. Rachel was at the meeting when they first called for volunteers. A cute butch plainly explained the risks. Rachel had never been arrested before but she started crying and laughing and said, "Sure, I'll do it, I don't give a shit," and something in her tone and the way her trans body shuddered caused the butch to look right at her and say, "No. Please don't."

———

The pogroms of May 2021. Around three hundred Palestinians die.

Rachel dreams of being gassed to death. In the daylight hours, her lungs burn. At the protest, everyone stays away from her because her dry cough sounds like COVID.

———

The Gazan genocide, October 2023 through present.

Rachel is at one of many protests—she's lost count. Aiden is home with Ezra. She insisted that she'd be okay on her own. It's a global warm-ily hot day, but she's wearing long sleeves to cover the burns and an N95 to protect people from her coughing and to protect her face from photos. There's a drone flying overhead and she's trying not to make eye contact with it. She's sweaty and uncomfortable and her limbs hurt. There's the usual deep, dull pain, a product of years of getting hate-crimed in her sleep. And there's new, fresh injuries as well.

A Palestinian is speaking. Rachel has by this point heard countless firsthand accounts from Palestinians who have lost their families, again, who have cousins buried under rubble, again, whose corpses are in ice cream trucks, again, who don't know which family members are still alive. After the speech, the crowd starts marching to the JFK building to get some people pointlessly arrested, again, and demand a ceasefire, again, as if Elizabeth fucking Warren gives a shit about their demands.

There are thousands of screaming, despairing people. Never again means never again. From the River to the Sea Palestine will be Free. Free free free Palestine. What do we want? Justice. When do we want it? Now. Intifada intifada. Some loud men to her right are trying to reappropriate a Vietnam-era chant, replacing L-B-J with Joe-Bi-Den, and it's not working. She passes by a lone, defiant Zionist on the sidelines holding a sign that says FREE THE HOSTAGES. Another guy of ambiguous allegiance holds a sign that says READ GLENN GREENWALD.

Seemingly everyone wants to assign blame. It's the settler colonialists' fault (correct). It's America's fault (correct). It's both sides (wrong). It's Hamas, who are literally Nazis. It's all Palestinians, who are all Nazis. It's the Israeli government, literally Nazi Germany. It's Netanyahu, literally Hitler. It's Biden, literally Hitler. It's somehow Trump, whom everyone knows is literally Hitler. The school administrators who suspend student groups because saying the word "intifada" on campus is equivalent to Nazism are themselves Nazis. The Zionists are acting on their cultural trauma instead of with compassion, which makes them literally Nazis. This is why no one wants to talk about the Holocaust with Rachel. Nearly a century of comparing literally every atrocity to Nazism has saturated public and private discourse. Rachel's queer kheverim always try to emphasize Palestinian narratives and voices. We are constantly, in every waking moment, grieving the tens of thousands of murdered Palestinians. We are also bracing for the day when this fucking country finally turns on us and the Jews devour their own, but it's too embarrassing to actually say it. Only the Zionists actually say it.

On the night of October 7, Aiden and Rachel read the news and Aiden unilaterally declares that he will sleep on the couch and tend to Rachel's injuries in the morning. Rachel's dream is the same every night, and it's now strictly linear. The Nazis break down the door of her home—not someone else's home anymore—and beat her until she stops resisting. They see her in a dress, a degenerate Communist homosexual Jew, and almost shoot her then and there but the man with the gun loses his nerve and angrily drags her out of the house. She doesn't make a sound. They threaten her until she stands up and march her through the streets to the train station and onto the train. It's a cool evening. The train is packed with Jews. The door shuts. She stands in shit for a few days. The doors open. She's marched to the gas chamber. She breathes in the rat poison. And she doesn't die, because this is a dream, and even in some of the most fucked-up dreams you're still beyond death. But she doesn't live either. She gets thrown into a heap with the corpses in a pit dug by Sonderkommandos. The corpses, and her living body, are set ablaze, and that's when she wakes up. Then Aiden wakes up, and he applies ice to her bruises and realigns the splint on the hairline fracture on her arm and applies antiseptic cream and bandages on the burns while Rachel weeps and checks her phone to learn how many Palestinians have died since the last time she checked her phone, how much of Gaza no longer exists, how many more Zionists are salivating at the chance to build settlements, which hospitals still have electricity, how long the communications blackout has lasted, how many journalists have died, how many children have been executed.

When the ground invasion begins, Rachel's screams are so loud that someone in the building calls the cops. Aiden and

Rachel assure them that it was just a bad dream, but cops continue to circle the building at night. At least, that's how it is for the first few nights. But then it stops always being the cops. Rachel can tell when she peeks through the blinds to look at their uniforms. Sometimes it's American cops. Sometimes it's German Nazis. Sometimes it's Israeli soldiers monitoring a dissenting self-hating Jew, an enemy of the state and its people. Ezra knows something's wrong, but he's too young to articulate the question or to understand the answer. To prove to herself and others that she's not crazy, Rachel takes some photos. They are terrible nighttime photos, but the regalia is still obvious and clear. She talks to her closest Jewish friends, who first blush and look at the floor before Rachel shoves the phone in their faces and makes them see. It doesn't make any sense to them but two of them volunteer to take shifts. That night they watch German Nazis watch their friend's house. This is real, they realize. But no one knows what to do about it because in the real world this is just how things work now.

Rachel's in bad shape. She's frail. She's learning how to walk with a cane. Her hair has gone white. She's forty years old but looks much older. When she loses her job for being an anti-Semite, she starts going to as many protests as she can because, like, fuck it, I guess.

Rachel finally remembers the Star of David and the chain. She can't remember the name of the campsite. She tries to contact Long and learns that he died of a drug overdose a few years ago. She had no idea. She tries Ellen, whom she fell out of touch with a long time ago. Ellen is the sort of autistic queer who doesn't need to ask for more context and immediately gives Rachel the location. Rachel checks the map. There are six campsites in a ring. She has no idea which one she was at, so she checks behind the restroom of each of them. She doesn't find the necklace because guess what there's lots of rocks and guess what she doesn't remember which rock and guess what she was high and she dug at the ground with her foot. Maybe someone in the past twenty years found it and took it. Maybe a crow spotted something shiny and gave it to a human friend.

Her phone has decided to start giving her push notifications of Al Jazeera's latest casualty count and she can't figure out how to get it to stop. She drives back from the campsite with the GPS on and has to periodically swipe away the friendly reminders. Every hour, fifteen Palestinians die, and the assault on Rafah hasn't even started. At home, she tries meditating to find inner calm but then her phone decides to start sending her push notifications to remind her to meditate. She swipes them away while IDF soldiers silently watch her apartment window. She takes long deep breaths with her blistered lungs. She considers doing something that she won't empower with a name and decides not to. Her friends are beautiful and wonderful and they periodically go to her house to check in with her. They hug her gently while Rachel silently reminisces about Nora's strength. She later tells Aiden about that night, and the roleplay she never asked for. Aiden has topped her in innumerable fucked-up scenes but this is too much. Rachel gets drunk and cries and thinks, well, maybe the past doesn't have any answers for us. The next morning, she has a black eye and broken teeth.

A few days after the emergency dentist visit, she picks up Ezra from school and drives to Revere Beach. Ezra is telling her about their new best friend's neopronouns but their speech is so slurry that she has no idea what they're saying. She asks them to repeat a few times before accepting that this is just going to be an unanswerable mystery until she meets the parents. Ezra then asks, "Why are you a girl?"

Rachel, driving, glances at the backseat in the mirror and says, "When I was your age, everyone thought they were a boy or a girl, even though some of them weren't." This isn't really true but it feels too complicated to explain how her identity changed as she accessed more nuanced language.

"Are you sometimes not a girl?" Ezra asks.

"Sometimes," Rachel reluctantly concedes, "but I think you'll have to teach me how to talk about it."

"Oh, it's easy," Ezra says. "You just ask."

They get to the beach. Rachel helps Ezra zip their coat back on. They look for seashells and Ezra asks questions about waves until they get tired and it's time to go home.

That night, as Gazans continue to be murdered, she has the same dream, only this time. Only this time. She escapes out of a window before the Nazis arrive. She runs through back alleys. She gets aboard a ship—it's not clear in the dream how this happens—and goes from one blood-soaked continent to another. She's one of the lucky few, in this dream. Absolutely everyone she has ever known dies but she, personally, is a descendant of those who lived. She moves to Boston. She starts HRT. She gets enmeshed in dyke drama. She gets really into synthesizers. She meets Aiden. She raises Ezra to be wiser than those who came before them. And then she wakes up to a dark iron-gray sky. Aiden is making coffee and for the first time in a long time, it feels like morning.

February 2024

Dedicated to the man I met at a protest who I'll never see again.

ASK A NECROMANCER: MORTUI VIVOS DOCENT

Amanda Downum

This April I attended my first RavenCon, my new local convention (and one of my favorite avian psychopomps). I was very excited to share the joy of death with a new audience. Here are a few of the questions I was asked.

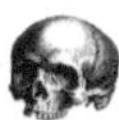

What's the licensing process moving state-to-state as a mortician?

So, you've graduated mortuary school, taken your local state law exam, and passed your National Board Exam. Congratulations! You're a licensed mortician. Now you want to move on, experience new places, new people, new corpses.

Specifics vary by state, but in general, the first thing you need to do is find a job. The days of embalming in your own basement are sadly* behind us. To be licensed in the field, one must be employed by a licensed funeral or mortuary establishment.

When you begin your job search, make sure to research state requirements—many states require periods of licensure in your original state before they will reciprocate, and some are longer than others. Louisiana requires at least one year; California requires three; Maryland requires five. New Mexico—which, when last I checked, had no in-state mortuary programs—does not have any time requirements.

---

* *My housemates and any plumber I may need to call are not sad.*

Once you find a job, you can then apply for a reciprocal license in your new state. You'll probably have to contact both the American Board of Funeral Service Education to have your National Board scores transferred and your original state's governing body to have your license verification sent over. Once that has been accomplished, you'll be eligible to take your new state's funeral law exam. Once you pass the law exam, you'll receive your new license.

The Texas law exam is pretty darn easy, by certain standards. It is—or was several years ago—online and open book. You receive the legal guide before you schedule the exam. The test is timed, however, and if you have not studied you are unlikely to find the correct information quickly enough.

Virginia, on the other hand, requires you to take your exam at a proctored testing center, with no notes available. And…who hurt you, Virginia? Why do you ask so many questions about pre-need contracts?[**]

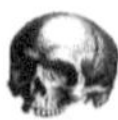

Two questions go hand in hand: Does embalming include reconstructive work, and what is your favorite part of the embalming process?

It does, and restorative work is often my favorite part of the job. The amount done varies by the embalmer's comfort and skill level, but Restorative Art is a major component of most funeral service programs. This ranges from using cosmetics to mimic natural color, to sculpting a nose or ear out of wax, to piecing a skull together like a jigsaw puzzle and then stitching up the skin on top of it.

The two leading causes of jigsaw skull and dental floss sutures, in my professional experience, are gunshot wounds and motorcycle accidents. Suicide and gun violence are their own

---

[**] *There is a reason, of course. There is always a specific reason when laws like this are passed.*

serious issues, but dammit, people, don't be stupid on a motor-cycle. At high enough speeds, a helmet does not stop your skull from shattering, let me assure you.

Jigsaw skulls are miserable work, and I have a permanent ache in my right hand these days. (Yes, I see a physical thera-pist.) But piecing a calvarium back together and then repairing the face on top of it is one of the most satisfying feelings I've ever experienced. There is no fixing this unfixable event, but making a person recognizable again is a powerful thing.

Are there red flags for identifying an unscrupulous funeral home, and by extension, can you say "I'm taking my business (and dead body) elsewhere?"

The biggest red flags I can think of are a funeral director trying to pressure you into something, or saying that some-thing—often embalming—is legally required. Embalming is not required by law in any state that I know of, except in cases where refrigeration is not available. Also, a casket is not required for cremation. If you want to have a public vis-itation with an open casket, then a funeral home can require embalming; cemeteries may also require it for mausoleum en-tombment. Pricing should be very clear, and by law the funeral director needs to give you their price lists up front.

Most of the directors I know will work with families to the best of their ability. Sometimes I wish they would say "no" more often. (Say no to tube tops; say no to 24-hour turnarounds; say no to letting someone sit in our cooler for six months and then asking us to get them dressed.) Prices are frequently horrific, as I've mentioned before, but there should be no hidden fees or upcharges, and families are not required to purchase anything they don't want.

And yes, you can absolutely take your business elsewhere. A funeral home cannot hold a body hostage.

Can we sit in on your class?

I would love to invite you, but the college might frown on it. For those of you who missed my last State of the Necromancer address, through a truly serendipitous chain of events, I am now employed as a professor at my local mortuary program. I'm as giddy as a schoolgirl. (Wednesday Addams, at least.)

And via our portal to the void, Aria asks: *Hi, what do you think will happen after the light shuts? Or what do you hope will happen after we die?*

My answer remains, I don't know, and I'm fine with not knowing. I grew up believing in the human soul, and in a vague notion of reincarnation. It has become harder and harder for me to believe in the soul as any sort of foundational identity, however, the more I learn about human brains. And while I try not to discount other people's experiences, I myself have never witnessed anything that required a supernatural explanation.

On the other hand, caring for the dead is profoundly important to me, in a way I can only describe as spiritual. Any funeral director will tell you that funerals are for the living, and that we do what we do for the families. But in my heart, that's not why I do it. I still hope there is some new adventure on the other side. But if it's just a beautiful, peaceful nothing, I'm okay with that too.

And finally, an anonymous shade writes: *One of my aunts passed away when I was a teenager, and I still remember seeing the dress she would be buried in hanging in our kitchen after*

my mother pressed it, awaiting the trip to the mortician. It was such a strange feeling to realize that this was not the last thing she ever wore. Instead, this is what her corpse would wear. That somehow made it feel even more important. During the viewing, the body in the casket did not look like my aunt to me, but her dress was so vivid, so real. Do families ever tell you why they have chosen the clothes they pick for their loved ones? What other kinds of things do families sometimes leave for you to include in their loved ones' final viewings?

Families do tell us stories about clothes and other grave goods, though I don't hear these stories often. Sometimes the narrative seems obvious—military uniforms, sports memorabilia, stuffed animals worn real with love. Other items are inexplicable without context. Photos and letters are common inclusions, as are cigarettes and candy. I've seen all kinds of keepsakes placed in caskets after a visitation.

If the person is being buried, anything that fits in the casket is welcome to be interred with them. In the case of cremation, there are limitations. We frequently cremate people with incense, money, extra sets of "traveling clothes." We recently cremated someone with several pounds of loose leaf tea. (That was the nicest our dressing room has smelled in quite some time.) Metal or stone items, however, or anything that doesn't burn, a crematory may politely decline. Also, anything that explodes. Adding a bag of popcorn to your dad's cremation container is a harmless joke; adding shotgun shells is *not*.

If you have questions for the necromancer—Professor Necromancer now!—you can submit them through our portal or via social media.

Fiction

END-OF-LIFE

Lauren Ring

THE bicycle shed at the edge of Heaven was painted a different color every time Kitty saw it. She was used to the ever-shifting hue, even fond of it, but one day the shed turned green and stayed green. Concerned, she submitted a prayer ticket: a humble request for fire-engine red. The prayer fluttered skyward. The shed stayed green. From this evidence, Kitty concluded that God was dead.

In her experience, God was almost always an anonymous volunteer. He was usually some overeager coder from the flesh, zealous and alive and confident in the ideals of the open-source afterlife. For this instance of Heaven, God went by the handle of TimInParadise, and He had been relatively attentive to His digital ghosts. Their prayers were heard and eventually answered. Kitty had seen neglected Heavens before, with prayer-clogged skies like the horizon before a storm. She had seen eternal nights, evaporated lakes, even minds unspooled beyond salvation.

It was possible that He was just taking an exceptionally long vacation, but someone *always* wanted to change that shed. Besides, Kitty knew it was easier to repaint wood than to patch up memories or recalibrate the laws of physics in an aging instance. She had no way of knowing what other prayers remained unanswered. Even with the small chance that He had just gone off the grid for some ill-advised spiritual retreat before approving the latest repaint, or simply forgotten to pay His sacred electricity bill, Kitty had to assume that her afterlife had been forsaken.

No one else seemed to have realized their abandonment yet. Kitty left the green shed behind and wandered through the park that was her slice of Heaven, unsure of how to break the news. Children splashed through the shallows of the near-by lake, and their laughter rang like bells against the warm concrete of the endless sidewalk trails. Two old men played chess at a picnic table while a woman in faded jeans sketched the fierce concentration on their faces. The artist occasionally paused to swipe at something stuck in the middle of her page. In life, it would have been a speck of dust or a squashed gnat, but even pixels have to go somewhere when they die.

What could she even say? *God is dead, and no, I didn't kill Him?* No one here would believe either half of that sentence, not from her. Not after everything she'd done to get here. She kept to herself even more than she had in life, and couldn't name even half of her neighbors if she tried, but they all knew each other enough to know that she didn't belong.

Heaven as she knew it would survive for a good while longer, even without its God. If Kitty found Him quickly, the other ghosts might never notice more than a leaky atmosphere and some missing picnic tables. They might even mistake her actions for altruism and forgive her trespasses. That would be a perfectly acceptable side effect, but Kitty just wanted to find Him—*needed t*o find Him. God had made her a promise, and she intended to collect.

With confident, practiced motions that made up for her shaking hands, she unpicked the ontological seam that shimmered between two birch trees and stepped from her Heaven to the next.

The networked web of afterlives was fairly new in the grand scheme of things. On the coldest day in the warmest September of Kitty's life, a news digest in her inbox casually announced that the internet's dead finally outnumbered the living. Backups and archives and prototype uploaded minds filled storage as quickly as it could expand. These various ghosts rested in blessed read-only memory until the following year, when their slumber was disrupted.

"Obviously, we all want our loved ones to drift peacefully to the other side," the disruptor explained, straightening the collar of his starched shirt. "I personally would never dare to disturb a single megabyte of my grandmother, may she rest in peace, but… Well, it seems like our dearly departed tend to stick around for a while. Isn't giving back to society what they would have wanted? Who are we to take this opportunity away from them?"

And so the ghosts were put to work. Their heaven suddenly had a price tag, and they paid their way by turning their minds into time-shares, renting out processing power to whatever machine learning labeler or altcoin miner booked a slot. Some surviving relatives were alarmed at the thought of their loved ones being scraped into datasets like ashes into a monetized dustpan. Some found solace in imagining guardian angels behind each watchful appliance, or convinced themselves they would be able to recognize each contribution to the automated choir: no longer just Siri reading out street names, but a late fiancée guiding her widow home. Most, overwhelmed by grief and funeral expenses, signed the consent-to-sale form without ever reading it.

And, of course, there were the holdouts.

———

Kitty, an inveterate holdout, walked the thread-thin tightrope between two Heavens and contemplated her options. Only a few of the debug shortcuts from her time as a coder in the flesh still functioned, leaving paths to slip between instances and not much more. It would have to be enough. The customized halos and bespoke pearly gates of the premium afterlife wouldn't suit Him any more than they suited her. She would find him in one open-source instance or another, and she would retrieve her rightful blessing by any means necessary.

The tightrope became a beam. The beam became scaffolding, the scaffolding became solid ground, and the solid ground became the endless sidewalks of an identically idyllic park. A strange, dissonant humming noise dripped through a crack in the firmament, located somewhere over the lake. Kitty stretched as languidly as her namesake and took in the familiar scenery.

These free Heavens were supposed to be temporary stopping points for open-source ghosts—the holdouts—while they designed a better afterlife together. Someone had chosen a park from their hometown as a placeholder until consensus could be reached. That was still ostensibly the plan, but no one could agree on anything without years of debate, and it took a whole volunteer God just to keep each simple park running. If a paradise had been built other than heaven itself, the corporate pay-to-play afterlife, Kitty hadn't heard of it.

Unlike Kitty's own Heaven, though, this park was empty. She wandered the sidewalks until the sun dipped low toward dusk, then flickered and rewound itself back to midafternoon. A string of afterimages trailed behind it and pulled a dozen strange shadows from each tree.

There was no noise but the humming of the fractured air. There was no movement but Kitty and the sun. Even the lake was still as glass. If there had ever been ghosts here, they were gone now, without even a queue of prayers to mark their passage. There was nothing she could learn from these crumbling remnants.

Kitty climbed the gentle slope of the tallest hill and lay back on the trampled-soft grass, trying to ignore the first tendrils of panic forming in her mind. From this angle all she could see was empty sky, as bright and blue as death. She lifted her chin in silent prayer.

If there's anyone out there—some savior of the pure, the ruler of this universe, a maintainer of the afterlife—please hear my merge request. This branch has withered beyond repair.

Could you please close this Heaven and transfer me to the nearest compatible instance?

The air began to heat up even as the breeze strengthened.

This, at least, made sense to Kitty. Heat and power were as intertwined as life and death. She had been God before, or played at it: ants under a magnifying glass, neglected fish tanks, abandoned friendships. Once—her life's biggest regret, if she got right down to it, even worse than the divorce—once she had forgotten her little spaniel, Morris, dozing below view in the back seat on a summer's afternoon. The emergency vet had been a small divinity in her own right, the cold metal exam table her altar and her warm hands an answered prayer. She had scolded Kitty even as she saved her dog. *He can't look out for himself! He relies on you, and you left him all alone!*

Yes, it was hot in Heaven today.

The third afterlife instance that Kitty crossed into wasn't empty, but she would have preferred that. This park was full of heat and noise and people, every square foot taken up by bodies and clutter, the soft grass entirely blotted out by endless picnic blankets and discarded jackets and drink coolers and backpacks and pizza boxes and parasols and bicycles and—

Kitty stumbled back, overwhelmed, and collided with an elderly woman. She was folding her picnic blanket into neat quarters, then shaking it out and starting over.

"Watch it, lady," she snapped. "Keep to your tile or I'll have to report you."

"To who?" Kitty asked, but the woman had already turned to scold a toddler reaching across from another bordering tile.

The toddler was young to be dead, but even younger to be in a Heaven. Maybe he was the child of an employee too stubborn for the main instance but informed enough to plan. Maybe upload norms had changed since Kitty passed, and backups were as regularly paced as vaccinations. She didn't know how long she had sat in the grass. Days and decades ran together without a God to keep minds tethered.

The biggest regret of Kitty's life was leaving Morris in her car, but the biggest regret of her death was leaving her mind on file. She had been confident at first, when heaven seemed within reach, but had stopped keeping up with uploads as news from the uplifted slowed to a trickle. They were too busy working to talk to their loved ones. This Heaven was nothing more than another eternally half-built circle of development hell, and she had damned herself right into it with her failsafe backups.

Kitty abandoned the tile she had instantiated on and shoved her way through the crowd in the approximate direction of the bike shed. It was slow going, but after only a few turns she could see it: an erratic, psychedelic strobe light of a structure, with dizzying patterns that resolved themselves into shifting squares as she approached.

Every ghost controlled their own tile and their own chip of paint. Thousands of small gods, clinging to their power as if it would lead them anywhere. It was Heaven by committee.

Her God wasn't here, and she would never find Him at this rate. The latticework of the afterlives was both more connected and more haphazard than she had realized. There was only one place left to go that might have the answers, so Kitty marched down the shortest route to the tallest tree, ignoring the complaints of the tile denizens.

She climbed to the treetop, and then kept climbing. From this vantage point, the ghost tiles looked more like patches on a quilt, and the bicycle shed was a tiny pin upon which angels danced. She climbed until she reached the thin glow of the sun, no brighter than it had been on the grass or by the lake. It was hotter, though. Much hotter. Kitty pulled herself through that golden lid and burned through to heaven.

———

The premium heaven had none of the customized halos that Kitty had expected. It had no swaying palm trees, no pearly gates, no hazy neon arcades. The expensive Heaven, heaven with a lowercase H, the one everyone thought of in the same genericized terms as velcro and xerox, was a park.

It was a park with tall birch trees. It was a park with a nearby lake. It was a park with gently curving sidewalks and picnic tables and soft grassy hills. It was a park with a bicycle shed, and the bicycle shed was unpainted wood. It was the same park Kitty had seen every single godforsaken day of her death. There was nothing better, nothing enviable, nothing even different. It had only ever been the walls between the Heavens that promised otherwise.

Kitty wasn't supposed to be in heaven, and every moment she was there drained funds from her withering estate. The contracted ghosts had no such concerns. They either sat perfectly frozen at long rows of picnic tables, their minds sent elsewhere for compressed eternities, or walked leisurely through the soft grass with sunlight in their hair. They were perfectly at peace, and every single one of them had a haunted stare that even their flawless avatars couldn't hide.

"Excuse me," Kitty tried, then lowered her voice when she realized she was the only person speaking in all of heaven. "Excuse me, I'm newly… I'm new here. Does anyone know if there's some sort of directory?"

At first, no one moved. Kitty cleared her throat and walked a few tables down the line. When she opened her mouth to repeat her plea, a young man on the sidewalk pulled her aside.

"Who are you looking for?" he asked, more hollow than gentle. "They've all forgotten how to speak by now, but I've only been here about a century of subjective time. I'll help you. I still remember what it's like to miss someone."

So heaven was different after all.

"I'm looking for my father," Kitty lied. "He always used the handle TimInParadise, and he was stubborn and old-fashioned. Can you find out if he's here or in one of the open-source instances?"

"I can only see heaven from here, but I'll try to find him for you. Hold on." The man stood terribly still without moving or blinking, then spoke again— "He's not here. I checked the whole roster, and the next hundred thousand in the queue."

Kitty's simulated heart dropped.

"Maybe he's using another name?" she asked, but the man was already frozen again, and this time he wasn't snapping out of it. Not that it mattered. He wasn't using another name. Kitty had known the truth from her first gut instinct, and had torn through Heaven after Heaven to hide from that knowledge.

God was dead. He was not backed up, or uploaded, or digitally preserved in any way. He wasn't in any of these nesting afterlife-shells and He never would be, and Kitty was seized with such violent jealousy that she felt she might catch fire.

"He *promised*," she wailed as her bank account ran dry and heaven shunted her out.

––––––––––

Back in her own park, Kitty reluctantly turned to the records from the flesh. There was a shortcut buried where the sidewalk curved left, then right, then left again. She knelt against the sun-warmed path and pulled dandelion fluff in precise combinations until a window like a prayer opened behind her eyes. Information scrolled past faster than she could think, but Kitty gritted her teeth at the dizzying feed and focused even harder. Heat and nausea washed over her. It took some searching, but eventually she connected God's username with His obituary. Sweat dripped from her brow as she sat back and read.

God's name turned out to be Timothy. He was nineteen, lived with his parents, and had always planned to have his mind backed up "later." That remained his plan right up until a downed power line sent fire sweeping through his bone-dry town. If he had thought of a heaven in his last moments, it was not Kitty's Heaven.

He had promised her eternal peace, and it was easier to blame a flawed God than a frightened boy with lungs full of smoke. It was easier to be angry. She had wanted to be innocent, like little Morris, a victim of circumstance whose only duty was to be nursed back to health with cool washcloths. She had wanted to confront God in His Heaven and demand the oblivion she was owed.

But Timothy never made it to heaven. Even if he did try to keep his word and delete her… Time moved differently here, lagging and speeding on parallel tracks, and Kitty didn't know how long it had been between his promise and his death. A month? A minute?

The sun shone on, relentless and serene. Nearby ghosts turned to Kitty in concern, and she realized she was sobbing, breathing only in great hitching gasps that left her faint. The breeze was gone. The air sat hot and still.

Someone was saying something to her. All Kitty could hear was the humming that had replaced her pulse. The heat was unbearable. She stumbled to the forest in desperate pursuit of shade and found only trees and harsh sunlight. She pushed herself forward, to the edge, and still there was no respite.

At her fingertips lay the seam of the world. Kitty had given up on escaping through it long ago, since all paths led to Heaven one way or another, but she was desperate now. She clawed the seam open. That wasn't enough. She scrabbled at the edges of the simulation until they frayed and tore. One bright thread burned her hand like a live wire, so she held tight to it and pulled hard.

The sun unraveled into her hands. A chasm yawned behind it and poured out clouds: several hundred copies of the same wispy cirrus, distributed in a perfect grid.

This glitch was much easier to notice than a bike shed that stayed green. People began to gather on the spiraling sidewalk, murmuring among themselves. Kitty, chest heaving, hands full of fire, lay flat in the dry grass and watched the clouds. If she squinted just right, she could see through the broken sky. Another park spread out, above her as if it was below her. Their bike shed was blue. A thousand ghosts looked back at Kitty, all of them weeping.

Surely something so massive, so important, so irreplaceable, had redundancies and shared knowledge. Surely the vault of the Heavens was not suspended by a single thread.

Kitty's first death had been of a prolonged wasting disease that she did not like to remember. This time, there was no slow fading out. There was only the heat of a body, the heat of a crowd, the heat of the summer, the heat of a star, all collapsing into each other recursively, a dizzying tunnel spiraling through infinity.

Then there was the sky split wide open, and then there were unheard prayers scattered like bright sparks from a spitting flame, and then there was only the cool darkness of the lake. Only an empty shed and the winter wind beginning to whistle through a sea of trees.

Poetry

THE HANDSOME MEN

Richard Leis

I dance with the handsome men I do not know
the music alive between their thighs, their liquid

skin and hard muscles, my feet and the floor
up my spine, into our shaking, sweating, swimming

pretty heads… My bladder aches. On the way to the men's room
a handsome man I do not know slaps my butt as he passes by.

You should smile more. I am shy at the urinal trough.
A handsome man I do not know slurs and tells me

You dance strangely. He glances down at my social
anxiety. Rolls his eyes. *Learn to dance or stay home.*

Shoulder to shoulder, all the handsome men I do not know
laugh while they piss poisons away. Outside the panting

club, the handsome men I do not know call me *Faggot!*
and with fists they beat an understanding of identity

into me until my head rings with the bass of their hate,
hematomata, and the relentless losing of consciousness.

The opposite of life is not death, but lonely. No deeper cold
than the end spread out without end or touch, soundless

crashing waves of the infinite grinding existence into formlessness…
but then, out of this place without sensation, a stranger that gets it

snaps me back. In the hospital, my eyes open to a handsome
man I do not know, who tells me *You're honestly lucky*

to be alive! A miracle. Blessed. From the ocean bottom
of swelling and gauze, I swim up to his indecipherable

piercing voice. How strange I feel. Clumsy. Empty of air.
Without heart. From the wounds under the bandages,

from swollen lips and sharpened teeth, the infinite moist
malice that came back with me dribbles. I cannot be

restrained. I reach up and pull the handsome man I do not know
to my face. His eyes widen. I see nothing of myself in reflection.

No one is prepared for his screams. More handsome
men I do not know fall or flee. I howl after them to

Tell all the handsome men I am coming!
Tell them how strange I have become!

THREE THINGS THAT HAPPEN THE NIGHT MY DAD DIES

Isabel Cañas

THE night my dad dies, he's not my dad—he's fifteen years old, fluffy-haired and lean, and he's sneaking through the neighbor's backyard with a friend. They're on their way to play a prank on their little sisters' sleepover when he trips and runs into a trampoline. Snap, crackle, *pop!* deep in the dark of his abdomen. He feels gray, he goes to his dad, and as he rattles in the passenger seat on the way to the hospital, his heart stops.

I

The night my dad dies, he doesn't really know what happened until he's already back. His resurrection hits with a blast of pale light and trumpets and brassy choruses that no one in the hospital can pinpoint the source of. The neighbors make the trampoline that killed him a shrine. They light candles in a circle and watch them wink like fireflies through thick summer nights. They ask him for intercessions, which he grants, sometimes benevolently, sometimes resentfully. It is difficult to intercede on behalf of so many people, especially strangers. My dad learns the term *emotional labor* twenty-seven years before anyone else and, when he is an adult, he thinks twice before he buries a statue of St. Joseph in the back yard of the house he wants to sell.

II

The night my dad dies, he glimpses the color and shimmering movement of another dimension. He knows he can only choose one or the other; the other draws at him with gentle fingers, but then he sees his dad's glasses glinting in the fluorescent hospital lights, so he chooses our world. He keeps that glimpse of the other side with him, though. He becomes a painter. He does a lot of drugs, trying to find that other side while he is safely grounded in the world of the living. When his dad dies, he's less careful. Ayahuasca, LSD. After a few years, he cracks it: He can cross between worlds whenever he wants and carry messages back from the dead. He never charges for his services; he is not interested in money, this dad of mine. Then again, he's not my dad, because this one never finds or marries my mom. I remain a mote of energy flitting through the dark matter of the universe, no one's second thought or disappointment. Maybe we'll meet in that other dimension when he dies again. Maybe we'll like each other.

III

The night my dad dies, he sees the River Styx and the boatman. He slips his hands into his pockets and finds that he has no money. The boatman says to look under his tongue, that's where they usually put the fare. My dad sticks his tongue out; no dice. The boatman shrugs. *Guess you have to go back.* "Which way?" The boatman points. *There's a dog. She'll take you.* The dog leads him all the way to the hospital room, and when he wakes, my dad asks for the dog. His dad says that's the drugs talking, but in a week, when there is a dog up for adoption at the pound, my dad sees her and knows. *That one.* Her name is Tippy. My dad says it's because there's a white tip on the end of her tail, but really, it's because he had nothing to tip the boatman with. Everything else is the same: He goes to church and he meets my mom at the party of a mutual college friend and then eventually there are the five of us, but this dad always has pockets and pockets of loose change. It scatters across the front hall table, it jingles in his winter coats when he steps off the train, it accumulates in empty pickle jars in the kitchen and the garage. It drives my mother crazy. When she complains, he shrugs. *You never know when you're going to need it.*

This is what happens the night my dad dies: A long night in the hospital, pale faces, IV drips, sixteen sutures that heal without drama. A white scar straight up the center of his abdomen, which he later tells us is a shark bite, and we believe it for years. Whatever he saw the night he died, he tells no one. He tells himself it never happened. We are not allowed to play on trampolines. We are sent to a sleepaway summer camp that has no trampolines, where we go to daily Mass and daily confession and daily catechism, where we sing songs about sacraments and forgiveness and sometimes go canoeing when the drought's not too bad. We are pure of soul, baptized and unblemished, always ready for the Kingdom of God, because it turns out, you never know when you might trip into it.

AUTHOR BIOS

CHRIS PANATIER lives in Dallas, Texas, with his wife, daughter, and a fluctuating herd of animals resembling dogs (one is almost certainly a goat). He writes mostly short stories and novels, and also draws art for book covers and metal albums.

COREY FARRENKOPF lives on Cape Cod with his wife, Gabrielle, and works as a librarian. His short stories have been published in *Vastarien, SmokeLong Quarterly, The Southwest Review, Reckoning, Flash Fiction Online, Bourbon Penn,* and elsewhere. His debut novel, *Living in Cemeteries,* is out now. He is the fiction editor for the *Cape Cod Review.* Follow him on Twitter @CoreyFarrenkopf, TikTok @CoreyFarrenkopf, Instagram @Farrenkopf451, or on the web at CoreyFarrenkopf.com.

ABHINAV is a graduate student residing in Delhi. His poems have appeared in *The Bombay Literary Magazine, Chestnut Review, trampset, The Deadlands,* and *Gulmohur Quarterly,* among other forums.

KAY MABASA (she/her) is a Zimbabwean writer and poet who lives in the city of Bulawayo, known as the city of "Kings and Queens." She holds a BA in Publishing Studies. Kay has short stories and poems published (and forthcoming) in *Solarpunk Magazine, Brittle Paper, After Dinner Conversation,* and the *African Ghost Short Stories* anthology from Flame Tree Publishing. Kay is currently working on her debut horror novel. You can follow her on Twitter @kay_mabasa_ where she always follows back.

ELEORA RYAN is a writer, director, and translator who seeks to highlight the moments that make up art. She believes that art is more than the final product—it is every instance that led to the creation of the product. Her writing is aware of this and comments on its own production, bridging the gap between process and piece. Like most writers, Eleora's work is an attempt to understand the world and her place in it. For her personally, this comes from inquiries into hidden patterns and the connections between seemingly unrelated happenings. Her deepest hope in her writing is to offer something emphatically human—something with the ability to feel deeply personal for anyone and everyone who engages with it, while adding something worthwhile to the conversations that matter.

STEPHEN KEARSE is the author of *Liquid Snakes* and *In the Heat of the Light*. His essays and reporting have been published by *The New York Times*, *The Atlantic*, *NPR*, *The Nation*, and other outlets.

ALI TROTTA is a poet, writer, editor, word-nerd, and unapologetic coffee addict. Her poetry has been published in *Uncanny*, *The Magazine of Fantasy & Science Fiction*, *Asimov's*, *Small Wonders*, *The Deadlands*, *Fireside*, *Strange Horizons*, *Cicada*, *Nightmare*, *Mermaids Monthly*, and several of the Rhysling anthology compilations. You can follow her on Bluesky (@alwayscoffee) or Instagram (@alwayscoffee7).

ESTHER ALTER is a trans anti-Zionist Jewish writer, game designer, and open source software programmer. Her fiction and poetry can be found in *Baffling Magazine*, *khōréō*, and *Reckoning*. Her games can be found on https://subalterngames.itch.io. Her open-source projects can be found on https://github.com/subalterngames. Follow her @esther_alter@mastodon.social.

LAUREN RING (she/her) is a perpetually tired Jewish lesbian who writes about possible futures, for better or for worse. She is a World Fantasy Award winner and Nebula finalist, and her short fiction can be found in venues such as *F&SF, Nature,* and *Lightspeed.* When she isn't writing speculative fiction, she is most likely working on a digital painting or attending to the many needs of her cat, Moomin.

RICHARD LEIS has been published in *The Magazine of Fantasy & Science Fiction, Star*Line, Eye to the Telescope, The Molotov Cocktail,* and anthologies from House of Zolo and Crone Girls Press. He works at the University of Arizona with the HiRISE team, which has had a camera in orbit around Mars since 2006. His website is richardleis.com.

ISABEL CAÑAS is a Bram Stoker Award–nominated Mexican American writer and graduate of the Clarion West and Odyssey workshops. She holds a doctorate in Near Eastern Languages and Civilizations from the University of Chicago. Her novels *The Hacienda* and *Vampires of El Norte* are out now. To find out more, visit isabelcanas.com.

STAFF BIOS

SEAN MARKEY publishes websites for a living and has always dreamed of publishing a magazine (about Death). He lives with his wife, Beth, in an old central Vermont farmhouse. Follow Sean on Twitter @PsychopompCom (if you want).

E. CATHERINE TOBLER is a writer and editor. You might know her editing work from *Shimmer Magazine.* You might know her writing from *Clarkesworld, Lightspeed,* and *Apex Magazine.* A trebuchet and Oxford comma enthusiast, she enjoys gelato and beer in her free time. Leo sun, Taurus moon. You can find her on Bluesky @ect.bsky.social.

NICASIO ANDRES REED is a writer, poet, and essayist whose work has appeared in venues such as *Shimmer, Fireside, Lightspeed,* and *Uncanny Magazine.* He's read slush for *Strange Horizons,* edited manuscripts for award-winning authors, and owns five different copies of *Moby Dick.* He lives with his family in Cavite province in the Philippines.

INKSHARK is a scandalously queer illustrator, author, and editor who lives in the rainy wilds of the Pacific Northwest. He enjoys exploring with his dogs, writing impossible things, and painting what he shouldn't. When his current meatshell begins to decay, he'd like science to put his brain into a giant killer octopus body with which he promises to be responsible and not even slightly shipwrecky. Pinky swear.

DAVID GILMORE is a writer, reader, and editor out of St. Louis, MO. His work has been featured in *The Rumpus* and at Lindenwood University, where he also received his MFA. He lives with his wife and son and spends his free time manning a stall in the Goblin Market selling directions to various Underworlds in exchange for rumors and information on where he can find his muse.

AMANDA DOWNUM is the author of *The Necromancer Chronicles, Dreams of Shreds & Tatters,* and the World Fantasy Award-nominated collection *Still So Strange.* Not content with armchair necromancy, she is also a licensed mortician. She lives in Austin, TX, with an invisible cat. You can summon her at a crossroads at midnight on the night of a new moon, or find her on Twitter as @stillsostrange.

LAURA BLACKWELL is a freelance editor and Pushcart-nominated writer. Her publications include *Chiral Mad 5, Nightmare,* and the *Aseptic and Faintly Sadistic* anthology. You can follow her on Bluesky, Instagram, and Twitter @pronouncedlahra and visit her website at pronouncedlahra.com.

CHRISTINE M. SCOTT has been a professional graphic designer, website developer, and brand consultant for more than twenty-five years. She is the creative director and copublisher of Nosetouch Press and has coedited seven anthologies, including the folk horror anthology trilogy *The Fiends in the Furrows.* She is also an artist and craftsperson—several of her handcrafted items were included in *Game of Thrones: The Compendium,* printed by Chronicle Books for HBO. For a complete list of her pursuits, please visit christinemariescott.com.

FELICIA MARTÍNEZ is a writer and artist born and raised in Eastern New Mexico, though home is now the San Francisco Bay Area. She is a 2023 Dream Foundry Contest for Emerging Writers finalist, an honor she achieved with a beloved work of flash. Find her on Bluesky and Instagram as @feliciafm.